THE PRECIOUS LIFE

Also by Che Parker

The Tragic Flaw

THE PRECIOUS LIFE

CHE PARKER

SBI

STREBOR BOOKS

NEW YORK LONDON TORONTO SYDNEY

Strebor Books
P.O. Box 6505
Largo, MD 20792
http://www.streborbooks.com

This book is a work of fiction. Names, characters, places and incidents are products of the author's imagination or are used fictitiously. Any resemblance to actual events or locales or persons, living or dead, is entirely coincidental.

ISBN-13 978-1-59309-210-8
ISBN-10 1-59309-210-5
LCCN 2008937809

First Strebor Books trade paperback edition December 2008

Cover design: www.mariondesigns.com
Cover photograph: © Keith Saunders/Marion Designs

10 9 8 7 6 5 4 3 2 1

Manufactured in the United States of America

For information regarding special discounts for bulk purchases, please contact Simon & Schuster Special Sales at 1-800-456-6798 or business@simonandschuster.com

DEDICATION

This book is dedicated to everyone who has touched
my life and blessed me with knowledge,
from the block to the board room.

ACKNOWLEDGMENTS

Thanks to my wife and best friend, Kristal Parker.
And to my daughter Sophia Parker,
the world's next great author

CHAPTER 1

AUGUST 15, 2008
12:51 A.M.

He wanted so badly to kill her, to give her the gift of eternity. Just end her life and be done with it. No more explaining where he was; no more questioning her whereabouts. He could be free. He could go out drinking and not worry about putting his ring back on. He could have as many women as he wanted. They wanted him, too, and if she was gone, he could have them all. He could stop wondering if his wife would catch him. He could stop wondering what she was doing, out with her friends, when he was at home. He could have a life. He just wanted to be done with the whole thing. This life. The life they had made. He wanted it to be over with. His heart was pumping fast now. No doubt hers was, too.

The bathroom was cold. Tiny goose bumps covered them both. Hers were wet. Thick humidity from outside seemed to claw at the windows. He spoke softly, pausing ever so briefly, between each word. He put so much care into the words he chose. Each syllable reverberated off the colorless bathroom tiles.

"Have you ever..." He stopped. "No. Fuck that. How many *times* have you cheated on me?"

His voice had always been deep. It seemed deeper now, though. More heavy, as if his pain weighed down his vocal cords, making them suffer the same punishment his heart was now enduring. His eyes were tightly shut. His dark hand ran smoothly over his eyelids, which felt like mushy flesh. There was still a pungent odor of bleach in the air.

"Kathryn! Answer me, goddamn it!" The volume caused her head to ache even more.

Soaked and terrified, Kathryn's thin frame shivered in the bathtub. Water crested halfway to the top. Sad black tears stained her face as the mascara loosened its grasp on the rim of her eyes. The silver sequins on her burgundy evening gown seemed to reflect her sorrow. The white of the bathroom surrounded them in an empty void. Gentle waves cascaded. Their reflections were displayed in it; ghostlike shadows swayed in the enclosed current.

"You filthy bitch! How many times have you cheated on me?"

Angered by her silence, he reached over and began to choke her. Strands of her hair stuck to the tile as he shoved her head under the water. It splashed out and soaked his gray T-shirt and shorts. She struggled for air. She fought. She struggled more. Her eyelids fluttered. Her tormented splattering was suddenly cut by a youthful sound.

"Uncle Josh," the child murmured at first, with a voice like maple syrup. She held her pink-and-yellow bath towel tightly. "Uncle Josh! No! Please, stop it! Please! You're hurting Aunt Kathryn!"

"Dawn! Go back to your room! Now, goddamn it!" Joshua demanded, never once loosening the vise on his wife's neck.

"Please, Joshua." Kathryn's voice was a faint whisper. "Dawn."

Joshua thought of his niece, her innocence. His face softened and he loosened his grip, releasing his wife from her watery confine. Dawn began crying and turned and ran toward her bedroom. The cartoon characters on her fluffy pink slippers seemed to weep as well as she slammed her door and dashed for the sanctuary of new rainbow-riddled blankets and sheets. She hid there, saying a child's prayer for her aunt and uncle. A little black dress and matching shoes lay where she left them a week ago. The announcement—a chubby face in black and white—was awkward next to the Dr. Seuss collection.

Joshua stared at Kathryn. He then knelt next to the bathtub, looking down at the floor. If someone had walked in at that moment, it would have looked as if he was praying to his wife. To this female god.

"We've been together for twelve years." His voice was low. "You're telling me you never once cheated on me? Kathryn, I'll fucking kill you right now. Why have you been coming home, like this?"

Joshua's mind suddenly left the swampy bathroom. He began to think about how beautiful his wife was. About the day he first saw her. About her radiant smile. It was only one of many reasons that had led to his deep infatuation for her.

He snapped back to the bathroom. On the sink was a glass dish where the bar of soap rested. Next to it was a glass container with more bars of soap. That was Kathryn's idea. Joshua wasn't much of a decorator, though he prided himself in critiquing what Kathryn did. He would often slide a vase two inches to the left, or rotate a pot of flowers so the greener leaves would show. He felt he was improving things. Kathryn felt he was being an asshole.

His knees ached from kneeling, so he propped his right foot up and leaned on the tub, resting his elbow on it and covering his face with this hand. He looked up at his wife. Sticky vapors clung to the windows.

Kathryn's wine-colored evening gown was drenched and clinging to her slim body. Her cheekbones protruded like jagged rocks. The blackness of her eye makeup had spread across her face in embarrassing concentric swirls. Sounds of the running water eerily coupled with the late-night news Joshua was watching before Kathryn stumbled through the door, inebriated and disheveled. The heel of her maroon stiletto was cracked.

"*Well, folks, don't expect any relief from today's high temperatures. The humidity we're feeling right now will continue throughout the night. It will increase tomorrow when daytime temperatures are expected to reach 95 degrees in parts of Virginia and southern Maryland. If you absolutely must be outdoors, be sure to drink plenty of fluids, preferably water.*"

Kathryn wiped her forehead with her left hand, then her right cheek and chin. The black makeup smudged her sculpted face. Her head throbbed. Then, suddenly, a facial muscle reacted. She smiled.

"What do you want from me, Josh?" It was a sweet and seductive voice, one with depth fit for an opera singer. "Haven't I been there for you? Supported you when no one else would? Rubbed your back when you were tired? I have never cheated on you."

Joshua looked away and began scratching his neck. The glow of the bathroom lighting made his moist face shine.

Kathryn laughed drunkenly, still intoxicated by the Pinot Noir she had been enjoying earlier.

"You don't love me. All that I have done for you." The words slithered past her once-perfect teeth, now showing signs of decay. "I don't know. Maybe it's because I've been drinking. I don't know. I gave you my heart a long time ago, Josh. And what did you do? You make me feel like shit. Don't act like you don't know why I've been coming home like this."

She wiped her face again. Shining lights illuminated the diamond on her finger, and the room momentarily bursts with a kaleidoscope of reds, blues and yellows.

"You know, Joshua. Joshua! Look at me! You know why!"

Joshua resentfully turned to face her.

"I would have done anything for you. Now, you know what I do, now?"

Joshua was silent.

"Now, every day, every fucking day, I hope, no, I pray, that you get hit by a fucking bus. That you get tangled up in a nasty pile-up on the Beltway and they need your fucking dental records to identify you. That's what I pray for, Joshua. Every day. Every day, that's what I fucking pray for!" She raised her voice and the water splashed.

Blood raced through his veins and Joshua was quickly on top of her, grabbing her throat and squeezing until her eyelids began to flicker like delirious candles. Kathryn gasped for air, nails scraping the tiled walls. The tub's faucet continued to spew hot water, which was now running down onto the floor and the white bathroom rug, turning Joshua's gray house shoes into a woolly soup. She struggled. His strength forced her to slide down the tile and back into the tub. Several sequins loosened from her gown and drowned in the whirling flood. Buckets worth spilled out onto the floor. The angel tattoo on her shoulder soaked in despair.

"I'll fucking kill you! You dirty fucking whore! Why have you done this to me? Why?!"

CHAPTER 2

JANUARY 2, 2005
4:38 A.M.

The sun had yet to grace the horizon but Joshua was already awake. Wearing his sweatpants and red collared shirt, he was fully dressed in the standard uniform. He usually arrived to work about ten 'til five, checked his schedule, and awaited the arrival of his first client.

"I give 'em two more weeks, tops," Chidu said. "To be honest with you, I'm surprised they lasted this long, you know?"

Joshua placed his gym bag in a locker. The room had yet to take on the smell of men and exertion. The tile and toilets still shined with a hint of disinfectant.

"Yeah, that's the New Year's resolution crowd," Joshua said. "They'll start thinning out in about ten to twelve days. Too bad, though. The extra money is nice."

"The extra broads are nice, too. Yo, when are you going to come to Nigeria with me? They will love you over there!" Chidu smiled. His bright white teeth sat in a perfectly straight row.

"You keep telling me that, Chidu, but I'm not sure. I don't know. What's it like over there? Do you guys have malls and stuff? You know? Is it a nice place for couples?"

"Are you fucking crazy? Couples? First of all, if you come with me, you're not bringing your fucking wife, boss. No way.

Do that shit on your own time, okay? And yes, we have fucking malls and drugs and pussy and gas-guzzling Hummers, too." Chidu smirked and tossed a towel in his locker. "Look, I know you're as black as me, but they love Americans over there! They'll hear your accent and jump all over you. Just tell them you're a rapper or something and they'll go wild! Trust me."

Joshua laughed and pushed his glasses up on his nose.

"A rapper? Really?"

"Yes, brotha, I'm telling you. I had three in one night last time I went home. Crazy! I'm telling you. Drinks, food, whatever you want."

"Okay. But I don't think I could afford a plane ticket to Nigeria. How expensive are they?

"You'll have to save up. I know money is tight for you. But, boss, we have to do it. And just one ticket. Don't be bringing your fucking wife. I promise you it will be the time of your life."

"I don't know. I want to travel and see the world and do things, but that stuff is expensive."

"Look, save up. I'll help you out if you don't have enough. Okay? After all, you know all a man wants in life, right?"

Joshua grinned.

"No, what is that?"

"To be treated like a king, boss. To be treated like a fucking king."

XXX

Out in the gym, the early-morning exercisers were already hard at it. Beads of sweat dropped on the carpet, the treadmill belts, the rubber matting, the hardwood studio floors. They ranged in age, mostly over forty, in search of the figure they had in high school and never appreciated. Joshua scanned the huge room for his client. He checked his watch. Susan was usually on time. A married mother of three, she had been the prom queen twenty years ago. Now, after baby number three, she was fat and her husband rarely touched her. She had hoped to change that. Then he spotted her. He waved at her.

"Hey, Josh, I'm so sorry I'm late, hon. How long have you been here?"

"It's okay. You walked right past me." He adjusted his glasses.

"Did I? I'm so sorry, hon. My mind is all over the place. We had a fight this morning."

"It's okay, Susan. I'm sorry to hear that. It does seem a bit early for fights, though."

"Well, not in the Anthony household. If warm bodies are present, it's a good time for a fight."

Joshua felt bad for her. Not that he felt her husband was a bad person, not at all. In fact, he could understand. But he felt Susan was a good person. She deserved better. Sure, she had gained some weight, but didn't they take vows? Vows that all married couples swore before men and before God to uphold until death?

"How 'bout we take that negative energy and make it positive? Let's work it on out."

Susan grinned and Joshua got her started on the dumbbells. She took hold of the weights—light, even by women's standards—and began squatting with them. She had noticed how her husband, Harold, always stared at young girls' asses. Tight and firm, her ass used to look that way, too. She needed it to look that way again. She was straining by the time she reached ten; a canal of perspiration ran down the middle of her back. Wrinkles on her forehead bunched like a wad of linen.

"You know how much I hate this shit, right?"

"I know, but Harold will enjoy it. Remember, that's our goal. Now give me five more."

Blaring from speakers above, old hip-hop lyrics played like a motivational soundtrack. Weights clanked as they were re-racked and a general whirling sound filled their ears. Bright overhead lamps illuminated rows of stationary bikes, elliptical machines, treadmills, and fleshy bodies eager to shed themselves of fat.

"Fuck Harold. From today on, I'm doing this for me. Why should he enjoy the benefits of my labor? Maybe some young hunk will want a piece of this."

Joshua smiled.

"You're right. Who needs Harold, anyway? Give me five more, then we can take a break."

Susan grunted out five more repetitions and dropped the dumbbells to the floor. She panted heavily, grabbing a hand towel and wiping her flush red face.

"Why am I in here torturing myself? How long has it been, Josh? A month? I should just get lipo."

"It's been a little over a month. Almost two, actually. And no, you don't need lipo. You're making great progress. It's funny, I remember the day I met you because the Redskins were in the playoffs. I was devastated because they lost in the first round to the Cowboys."

"Yes, I do recall that. You were definitely blue, kiddo. I thought about getting another trainer after that first day. I was thinking, *how the hell can this guy motivate me to get in shape when he acts like his puppy just got ran over?*"

"Really? You thought that?" Joshua laughed. "I wasn't that upset. Truth be known, I liked the Cowboys when I was younger. You know, America's team? But they made a few moves that I never forgave them for, so I was done with them. Ready for the next set?"

"Just about. Let me ask you something. You're married, right? I mean, I can see you wear a ring."

"Yes, I am. I've been married for five years now, but we've been together for about seven."

Susan took a deep breath and swept her dusty blond hair from her eyes. Half of it was caked to her head, adhered by perspiration.

"Only five years of marriage? Try fifteen. I asked because you seem really happy. How do you do it? Is there something I'm doing wrong? You guys have kids?"

Joshua took a sip from his bottled water.

"Not yet. I think my wife is ready. I'm not. But you know, things are going well. You just work at it. Every day isn't perfect, you know? She loves me and I love her. And I trust her with all my heart. I think that's the biggest thing. That's what my mother always taught me. To trust."

Susan bent down and held the weights again.

"I hear ya, kiddo. Trust is important. Harold has been fucking a coworker for over three years now. I've known since the beginning. Men are so stupid. They're sloppy. Don't cover their tracks well." She wiped her sweat again. "How's that for trust?"

Joshua felt embarrassed.

"I'm sorry to hear that. Maybe you just suspect something and nothing's really going on."

Susan looked up at him. Wrinkles lined her forehead as if she couldn't believe what she was hearing.

"Josh, receipts, credit card statements, e-mails. I didn't receive a dozen red roses or stay at the Marriott in Crystal City or eat at the Palms. Trust, you say? Trust is the bitch that will slit your throat in the dark."

Susan pounded out five more reps, then dropped the weights again, this time exhausted. Joshua went to hand her a bottle of water, but she waved him off. Around them, middle-aged professionals sweated and grunted and fretted for the bodies they either once had or had always wanted. Some wanted it for themselves; most wanted it for others.

⁂

"Hey, Josh, do you think you can have those workouts and fitness tests looked at before you leave today?" Rodrigo asked. "Corporate wants us to start offering more group classes. Just pack those fat bastards in there. Most of them are federal employees. You know that's where the money is? Not in that individual workout crap you're doing."

It was now five in the evening and Joshua had put in a long day's work of training clients and answering random questions from gym members and their guests. He was exhausted.

"Sure thing."

"Thanks, pal." Rodrigo tapped his clipboard and left.

Chidu, who had just finished training a client, overhead the conversation and slid into Joshua's office.

"Boss, tell Rodrigo to fuck himself. That's not your job."

Joshua placed a file in the desk drawer.

"I know. But Rachel normally reviews the group class workouts and she called in. Sick kid."

"Fuck that. Tell him to bring his ass out on the floor and train these sweaty, fat broads and these fun boys that smell like ass."

Joshua chuckled.

"It's okay. I don't mind."

Chidu took a quick look out the door.

"Fuck that. You don't know how to say no. Stand up for yourself. What if I asked you to wash my penis and my teabags? Would you?"

Joshua laughed. "Shut up, Chidu."

"But see, that's what I'm saying. You didn't say no. Stand up, boss."

A pair of slim Asian girls suddenly strolled past the office, smiling and waving at Chidu.

"You see that?" Chidu was giddy. "That's why I stay ready, so I don't have to get ready. Later, boss. Duty calls."

Joshua shook his head and sighed. He was ready to head home. He felt his cell phone vibrating against his hip. The number popped up. It was Kathryn.

"Hello."

"Hey, honey. What you doin'?"

"Finishing up some work. What's up? I miss you."

"Oh." Kathryn blushed and smiled. "I miss you, too. Just wanted to know what you want for dinner? I'm in the grocery store now."

He rubbed his forehead.

"It doesn't matter, honey. I know it'll be delicious, sweetie. That's one of the reasons why I married you."

Kathryn picked up a box and looked at it.

"Is there something wrong? You sound upset."

"I do? No, I'm fine. It's been a little busy at work. I'm kind of tired, too. Can I call you back?"

"Yeah. Sure. Oh, something is wrong with the microwave.

Whenever I put in a plate and start it, the clock goes blank. Maintenance might need to come in and look at it. I was talking to Roxanne the other day, and she said she had the same problem with the microwave in her apartment. She thinks maybe there's like a factory defect. She said they had the same model. I told her I wasn't so sure about that. Those types of things are usually reported in the news, right? Faulty electronics? I'm thinking they would probably issue a recall or something. Do you remember seeing anything in the paper? You read it on the train, right?

"No. No, I haven't seen anything."

"Oh. Well—"

"Hey, babe. Look. Can I call you back? I really need to finish up a few things."

"Oh, okay. Sure."

"And I think I'm going to be a little late for dinner. I have to look over a few things for Rodrigo."

"Oh, okay. I thought you weren't going to work those long hours anymore. You told me—"

"Yes, honey. You're absolutely right. I was supposed to be home by now, but the other group trainer called in sick. Her daughter is sick, or something. That's what she said, anyway."

"There's no one else there that can do it? You're going to be late for dinner, again. That's not right. You shouldn't have to be late for dinner with your wife."

"You know, unfortunately, there is no one else here who can do it. So I will see you tonight. An hour or so from now. Okay? I have to go. I have to finish up. Somebody in our house has to work."

Kathryn paused for a moment.

"Okay. See you tonight," she mumbled in a low voice.

Joshua pulled up the last few pages that needed to be reviewed.

"I love you."

There was silence on the other end.

"Josh. I said, I love you."

"Oh, yeah, babe. I love you, too. See you in a few."

XXX

When Joshua got home later that evening, his favorite movie, *Known Teeth Kingz*, had already been on a few minutes. He immediately grabbed his plate from the stove and copped a seat on the sofa in front of the television. The movie could come on ten times a week. Joshua would be in front of the set all ten times. Kathryn sat in the bedroom with the door closed.

Corporal Sanchez wiped the sweat from his brow. Just one hundred kilometers from their rendezvous, his company hunkered down for the night, bringing an end to the day's long march. The humidity quilted them.

"Sanchez. Yo, Sanchez! You still have that extra water ration? I'll give you double what you were asking for earlier."

Rodriguez was always thirsty, more so than the others. In boot camp he would drink his canteen dry and offer to do KP duty for extra rations. They said he never got adjusted to the new way of things. For Rodriguez, today was nearly unbearable, and he wasn't the only one: Several men had already been visited by the medic for severe dehydration.

"Man, J-Rod, no can do. Already got double from Jackson. Next time, act. Be decisive. Be a Marine!"

"Ooh-rah," a chorus erupted. Troops milled about, pulling rocks

from their boots, clearing the sand and dust from their weapons. Some thought about their girlfriends at home. Others jacked off in their sleeping bags with whatever remaining strength they had left.

"Jackson, let me get a sip of that H20," Rodriguez edged closer to Jackson's tent, resting his forearm at the apex of the triangle.

"Fuck off, Rod, man. Maybe after I drink this cube, you can suck my dick and extract the water from my tea bags."

Sanchez and Nguyen laughed. Their tents were just a few steps away.

"A, Nguyen. Nguyen!" Jackson called out.

"Que paso, my brotha?" Nguyen had a straight row of pearly white teeth.

"Man, what the fuck was that bitch yelling about in that village? Crazy, dumb-ass bitch."

"I do not know, my brotha. I speak Vietnamese, not Hanyu, or Mandarin, for that matter."

"Yeah, well, that screechy chicken talk was driving me crazy! We should have smoked her and that retarded kid of hers. Would have saved both them a lifetime of heartache. Well, at least a few more weeks at the way shit is going now. Won't be much longer till we smoke all these gooks. I mean, chinks. My bad, Nguyen."

"Hey, no problem, my brotha." Nguyen took a deep breath and blew the dust and sand from his helmet and wiped it with a rag. "I'm an American. Fuck 'em all."

"Ooh-rah." Jackson flashed a smile and reached for his ear buds.

Sanchez rolled out his sleeping bag and lay on his back, looking up at the colorless night sky. They had humped all day until they reached the village of Ltasa in the arid Quixwuan Province. It was suspected that the Chinese military, thwarted in the far eastern coastal cities, had regrouped and fortified the area villages with troops and artillery. When Echo Company reached Ltasa, all they found were old men with *paper-thin skin and old women with gray hair. One or two sympathizers mouthed out. That was enough for all the men in the village to be executed. The few younger ones who still possessed vitality were gunned down as they ran for the mountains.*

"You guys think we're going to win?"

Nguyen looked up from his wiping. Rodriguez glanced over from the rock he was sitting on. He had managed to score a ration of water for triple what Sanchez had originally asked.

"Sanchez, you starting that shit again?" Rodriguez shook his head. "Yo, Jackson! Yo, you black bastard! Sanny is talking that dumb shit, again."

Jackson yanked the buds from his ears.

"Can't you dumb motherfuckers see I'm trying to listen to my fucking music? Comprende*?"*

"Man, just tell your boy Sanny that we're going to win."

Jackson frowned. The camp lights struck the sweat on his forearm and illuminated the defined muscles that ran from his wrist to his elbow.

Joshua stood up and turned the television off. He rubbed his eyes. He had seen enough for today. He turned and went to bed. He noticed the bathroom door was still closed, but he paid it no mind.

CHAPTER 3

AUGUST 15, 2008
12:57 A.M.

Bubbles released through her mouth and out the water. The air vessels became fewer and smaller. They nearly stopped when Joshua abruptly ceased his attack. *Dawn*, he thought. His arms recoiled and he planted himself on the toilet, distraught. Kathryn sprung from the water, vacuuming for air. Waterlogged, dirty, blond curls rained down upon her nose, her prominent cheekbones.

Concerned and afraid, little Dawn frightfully peeked into the bathroom, ogled the water, the rage and black smudges on her aunt's face, and again disappeared into her room. There were several minutes of silence. The faucet continued to waterfall onto the floor.

"Why, Kathryn? Who were they?" His voice was low and contrite. "You know, I used to love you so much. So fuckin' much." Joshua's face was buried in his hands.

Kathryn looked at him with disgust.

"Who were they, Kathryn?!"

Her slim legs dangled over the bathtub's edge like soggy noodles. She smirked, exposing her teeth, one now chipped from the tumult.

"Who were they? Who were they? Joshua, honey, please get out of my fucking face."

Joshua looked at her. His chest rose and fell under his wet gray T-shirt.

"Kathryn, don't fucking lie to me. Not now. Not today. Don't do it. Don't fucking lie to me."

Teeth gnashed in Joshua's tightly closed mouth. He wanted so badly for things to be perfect. He didn't want to be here. Not like this.

"Look at us, Kathryn. We're not the same. You act different. You look different." He lowered his head. He stared at the floor. Water pooled near his feet. "Why are you doing this to me? To yourself?"

Kathryn smiled. "You want the truth, Josh? Can Joshua take the truth?" She smirked and ran a hand across her face.

Joshua frowned in revulsion. Nausea gurgled in his stomach.

"Where do you want me to start, Joshua? That day at the Pentagon? You know, I just felt so slow. So weak. I didn't think I was going to make it. I felt fat and helpless. I didn't like that feeling, Joshua. I didn't want to be the helpless person that couldn't save her own life. Like the person in the movie hanging over a ledge. If only they could pull themselves up, they'd live. Just pull and live."

Joshua let out a deep exhale. He scratched his neck.

"What else is there, Kathryn? I wasn't talking about that day."

She smirked, hurt that her pain failed to elicit any emotion from her husband. Not even a shred of sympathy. She responded in kind.

"What else is there? Let me see. Well, you weren't the best I've had, Joshua. Did you know that? I'm sure I told you you were. Right? You weren't. You were practically a fucking virgin when we met." She smiled. "It definitely seemed that way. I'm sorry, Joshua. I know men have this ego thing. You weren't my best. Did I cheat on you? Think about it. Think really hard about it. What do you think?"

CHAPTER 4

OCTOBER 17, 1988
6:48 P.M.

"Boy, you better hurry up. You betta not make me late for this parent-teacher conference." Joshua's mother blew out a smoky plume and mashed her cigarette into a full ashtray. She checked what appeared to be an old stain on the counter. "Did you spill some pop in here?"

"No, ma'am. I can't find my shoes!"

"Who are you yelling at? Have you lost your mind?"

Joshua was nervous. He purposely took his time. After a string of questionable incidents at school, he was afraid Mrs. Lockerbie would impart all the gruesome details to his mother. The consequences would be dreadful.

"I found them." He slid his glasses back on his nose.

"Come on. You didn't tear up that room, did you?"

"No, ma'am."

"Good. Come on."

✕✕✕

Joshua's mother was a stickler for being on time. That was something her father had instilled in her, and hence something she stressed with her only child. Timeliness and cleanliness. Those two elements were must-haves in Lorraine's household.

"You're not going to have me late. You want me to look like a fool in front of that white woman?"

"No, ma'am." Joshua stared out the window of his mother's car at the one-story homes that lined both sides of the avenue. He longed to live in one of them. Dim, yellow bulbs lit their front porches. Mothers and fathers made their way home from long days at work and began taking their seats at dinner tables.

"Because that's what they want, Joshua. They want you to fail. They want to put you in special ed classes and have you lookin' stupid. On a path to prison. But you ain't stupid. I know you're not stupid. And I know these first-quarter grades better be lookin' like As and Bs."

Joshua looked down and fumbled with the tape deck. His skinny fingers looked like dark twigs. Outside beacons of stars dotted the sky above the cold Midwestern autumn.

"You hear me talking to you? Boy, I'm talking about your future. You not gon' end up in somebody's jail. I'll kill you first. I mean that. Lord knows, I mean that."

XXX

Lorraine pulled her Ford up to the school, a long brick building with two stories of windows and a main entrance right in the middle. She checked her makeup in the window and gave her son a once-over.

"Come on. And you betta not have me embarrassed up in here. Is there anything I should know about before we walk in?"

Joshua shook his head.

"Are you sure? Boy, I will kill you if you have me up in here lookin' like a fool. Let's go."

XXX

The school was well lit for the year's first session of parent-teacher discussions. In all the years of Joshua's schooling, Lorraine had never missed one. Tonight, the halls and classrooms were filled with parents and their children, some walking hand in hand, others on the verge of tears. Joshua and Lorraine never held hands, so the best he could wish for was to not be on the verge of tears when it was time to head home. If he wasn't crying, it was a good night, he thought.

"Hello. Mrs. Lyon?" Josh's teacher extended her hand. Her freckles seemed more pronounced now that her summer color had faded.

"Hello. Actually, it's Ms. Williamson. Nice to meet you." Lorraine's hand swallowed hers.

"Oh, gosh. Sorry about that. I'm Mrs. Lockerbie, Joshua's teacher. Please, come in. Have a seat."

Lorraine smiled and Joshua slowly shuffled in behind her. Mrs. Lockerbie sat at the work table where earlier that day the students had prepared cards for their parents to read, if and when they visited. Lorraine saw the seats and frowned.

"I'm sorry. I don't think these seats will work for me." She laughed. "I'm afraid I'm not a little woman."

"Oh, oh, no. That's fine." Mrs. Lockerbie began to turn red. "Josh, can you go next door and get your mother a chair from the music room?"

Joshua promptly retrieved a chair and the discussion began. Mrs. Lockerbie laid it all out—Joshua's homework, his interactions with his classmates, his appearance ("always nicely pressed"), and his shyness. Lorraine took it all in.

"Now, I know I've been talking a lot. Do you have any questions for me? Overall, Joshua is a great kid. He's been doing much better since he started wearing glasses. He makes solid Cs, an occasional B. I think his shyness and his reluctance to show initiative are holding back his progress right now. With a little work, he could be a strong C-plus, maybe a B-minus student."

"Well, Mrs. Lockerbie, first I want to thank you for your time tonight. I know you have these children all day, and they must be driving you crazy. I don't see how you do it." Lorraine broke into laughter.

"I actually love kids. I love teaching and I love coming to work every day."

Lorraine frowned. "Really? That's interesting. Well, anyway, thank you. Joshua is a little shy. He's an only child and spends a lot of time by himself, mostly reading and drawing pictures. He really likes to draw pictures of houses. I guess that's because we live in an apartment. I caught him playing with himself a few times, and I think that might be affecting him, too."

Joshua, who up until that moment had been staring at the alphabet on the wall, suddenly looked stunned.

"Oh, uh, I see." Mrs. Lockerbie squirmed in her seat. "Well, I think that's normal at that age. Children tend to explore their bodies, and I think that's perfectly normal."

"Well, with all due respect, I wasn't raised like that, Mrs. Lockerbie. I don't think it's normal. I think it's a sin and he shouldn't be playing with himself all the time like that. I caught him one time with the Sears catalog, just staring at the underwear section. You should have seen the look in his eyes. Lustful."

"Mom, please." Joshua anxiously scratched his neck. He was two seconds away from running out the building and never looking back.

"Mrs., I mean, Ms. Williamson, again, research shows us that this is normal behavior. I really don't think you have too much to worry about. Joshua is a good kid. His grades are okay and he's a pleasure to be around. My inclination is that he will someday grow out of his shyness and really surprise us all. I'm sure of it."

Lorraine smiled and rocked back. The chair squeaked.

"Maybe you're right. I hope you're right. Joshua and I will have a conversation later about this. I do want to thank you for your time. You seem like a nice lady and I know Joshua's good behavior will continue. If you ever need me, or if Joshua ever acts up, please do not hesitate to call me."

"Okay. Well, now that you mention it, there was one thing. It's nothing major, just something I've noticed." Mrs. Lockerbie swept a lock of her red hair behind her ear.

"Nothing major? Okay. What is it?"

Joshua swallowed a block of spit and nervously scratched his neck.

"I've noticed that when Josh gets teased or doesn't do well on the playground, he takes it really hard. You can tell he's upset. No fights or anything like that. Like I said, nothing to be overly concerned about."

Lorraine adjusted her purse strap and exhaled a deep breath. A few children ran past in the eerily lit nighttime hallway.

"I see. Mrs. Lockerbie, in my household, I teach Joshua to stand up for himself. If someone hits him, he's taught to hit back. Now don't get me wrong. I told him to never start anything. Never! But if someone messes with him, then by all means, he has to defend himself."

"I understand. Yes, a lot of our parents have expressed that to me. And with all due respect, we would prefer it if the children report any problems to the teachers first. We wouldn't want anything to get out of control."

Lorraine shrugged and pulled the top of her blouse closer together. Mrs. Lockerbie smiled and looked up at the clock.

"It's getting a little late now, Ms. Williamson, and it's been a pleasure speaking with you." She glanced over at Joshua. "I'm sure I'll never need to contact your mother about anything. Right, Josh?"

The boy nodded.

"Good." Lorraine stood and extended her hand. "It was nice meeting you, Mrs. Lockerbie. You have a good night."

"Same to you. See you tomorrow, Josh."

5:30 P.M.

"What time does your daddy get home?"

"He won't be home until about seven. Why, Chico? Why you worried about it?"

"Yo' daddy ain't ever home. I'm just saying, baby girl." He eased closer to her. "You lookin' real sexy in those jeans. Got the bomb airbrush on 'em. You got those at the swap meet?"

Kathryn grinned.

"Yep. Off Slauson. Me and Roxanne went last week. You like 'em?"

"Heck yea, baby girl. I'd like 'em even more if they were on the floor. You feel me?"

"Whatever, boy."

Kathryn got up from the living room sofa and headed toward the kitchen. A window over the sink looked out on a beautiful day in southern California.

"You want something to drink? Some soda?"

"Naw. You got some beer? Like some Old English?"

Kathryn smirked and checked the fridge.

"Beer? Boy, you the same age as me. My dad would go off if he saw one of his beers missing."

"Please, girl. I'm grown. This is my house!"

Chico slammed a couch cushion on the floor, nearly toppling over a pile of old records stacked high above the coffee table, which itself was covered with old *Ebony* and *Jet* magazines, a car battery, and several ashtrays packed with cigarette butts.

"Where yo sister at?"

"Patrice? Who knows?" Kathryn said, moving a jar of pig ears to the side. The chill of the glass felt pleasant on her warm fingertips. "Probably with her boyfriend."

"Man. She ain't ever here, either." Chico spotted a stray dollar on the floor and quickly scooped it up and stuffed it in his pocket. "Yo' daddy don't care that she ain't ever here?"

"I guess not. He never says anything to her. She doesn't really stay out late. She and her boyfriend have been dating for a while. I guess they really like each other. He only came over here once. My daddy cursed him out. He's a cool guy, though. The other day—"

"Dang, girl. You are a talker! I didn't ask for all that." Chico laughed.

"Shut up, boy. Whatever."

Kathryn was finally able to find something to drink and she made her way back to the living room, stepping over a large ceramic Rottweiler and a couple empty beer cans.

"It's nasty up in this motherfucka. Yo' daddy don't clean?"

"Nope. He makes me clean, sometimes. My room is clean. That's all I care about." She stopped and looked at Chico. "Talkin' 'bout you grown. We both thirteen, so don't trip."

"Whatever, homey. Like I said, I'm grown up in here. Running this house and the rest of L.A. Me and my homeboys. Betta act like you know, blood."

Kathryn laughed.

"Yeah, right."

She sat down next to Chico with a cold can of Sunkist and took a drink. The weather outside was warm. A cool breeze blew. Sparse clouds lazily drifted through the sky.

"I'm saying, what the fuck is up with your sister's eye?"

Kathryn almost choked on her soda. She paused and clenched her jaw.

"What? Shut up, Chico!" She punched his arm as hard as she could. An orange droplet stained his red T-shirt. He didn't notice. "Nothing is wrong with her eye! That's not funny and it's not cool. She can't help that."

"Dang, girl. My fault. Why you trippin'? And where's my drink? And why is it so dang hot up in here?"

"My daddy won't let me turn the air on when he's gone."

"Dang. Open a window then!" Chico yelled. "Where is he, anyway?"

"At some meeting. You know I might be leaving Cali at the end of this semester. He wants to be closer to his mother in Maryland. He said she's dying."

"Maryland? Who the hell lives in Maryland?"

"I have a lot of family there. I've been once. I really don't remember it. You know this is going to ruin my chances to be famous. I'm supposed to be over in Hollywood, doing my thing!"

"Dang, baby girl. I'm sorry about that. So you might be leaving me? I guess we can't be wasting no more time, then, huh?"

Chico reached over and pulled Kathryn close and began kissing her. She resisted at first but the warmth and softness of the embrace pleased her. She responded by snaking her tongue in and out his mouth. Enjoying the moment, Chico leaned in and began caressing between her thighs.

"Dang, girl. Hey, let's go to your room." Chico squinted and smiled. "I'm saying, you got me all ready over here."

Kathryn thought for a moment. She looked at Chico's cornrows, the Old English tattoo of his arm. His older brothers and friends did run the neighborhood. He was cool. Funny. Cute. Tough.

"Okay."

Next door, the neighbor's pit bulls belched a chorus of grumbling barks and howls. Black bars covered the windows but the light that passed through brightened the hazel in Kathryn's eyes as she led Chico by the hand to her bedroom. Pink sheets and a pink sheer canopy draped the small bed while stuffed animals kept the pillows company.

Chico took a seat on the bed, pulling Kathryn on top of him.

They began kissing again, more touching now. More fondling now. But Chico wasn't satisfied with that.

"Are you going to kiss it for me?"

Kathryn pulled back and frowned.

"Kiss it? Naw, Chico. I've never done that before."

He kissed her neck.

"Baby girl, it's nothing. It's like licking a lollipop."

He smiled again and caressed her cheek.

"If you really like me, you'll do it. You like me, right?"

"Come on, Chico. You know I like you. But—"

"Okay then, Kat. Here."

She looked down and began to reach for it when she heard keys jingling outside the front door. Her heart skipped a beat.

"My daddy's home! You gotta get out!"

"Damn, blood. For real? Shoot. Where you want me to go?"

Kathryn frantically checked her clothes to make herself look presentable. Zipper was up. Shoes were on. Hair was okay. T-shirt was still tucked in.

"Look. The bars on this window are loose. Hurry!"

She quickly lifted up the window and the screen.

"Kathryn. Kathryn! You home?" Her father's voice was direct.

"Oh shit! You gotta get out, Chico! Slide the bars to the side. Hurry up!" She turned toward her door. "Yes! I'm here. Just lying down."

"Dang, baby. This is messed up. I'm finna' rip my khakis." Chico managed to squeeze his thin frame out the window between the bars and the siding. The neighbor's pit bulls ran to the fence and their chorus of barks and growls grew louder as Chico touched down a few feet from them on the opposite side.

"Kathryn! Come get ready to make dinner."

"I'll see you at school. Bye." Kathryn slowly moved the bars back into place and lowered the screen and the window. The dogs continued to bark along the length of fence, mirroring Chico's movement until he was no longer in sight. She again checked her appearance in her mirror and then walked into the kitchen where her daddy was waiting.

"You been in my 'frigerator? What I tell you about that? You gonna be fat like your mama was."

"Sorry, sir. I was thirsty."

"Drink water! That's why we have a faucet. You gonna be fat just like yo' mama. A fat pig. Where's Patrice? And where's dinner?"

Kathryn leaned against the kitchen's door frame.

"Patrice isn't here. I was doing some homework and—"

"Look, girl. I don't want to hear it. Just get dinner made."

Ledroit sat down on the sofa and unlaced his oxfords. "I put some chicken in the fridge to thaw. Should be ready by now. Go ahead and fry it up and make them potatoes, too."

Kathryn let out a low sigh.

"Yes, sir."

11:10 P.M.

"Light that cigarette for me. I want to talk to you." Lorraine walked to the bathroom and shut the door. She had roused Josh from his sleep. Something came to her in the night and it couldn't wait until the morning.

The boy rubbed his eyes, then grabbed the small box and pulled out a long brown cigarette. His hair was an uneven bush. He slid his tired feet over to the stove and turned the front burner on. Blue flames struck up. He put the cigarette in his mouth and took two short puffs. Lorraine taught him that more than two puffs and he'd be wasting her cigarettes. Two good puffs would always be enough.

"You light that cigarette?"

"Yes, ma'am." Joshua took a seat at the small round kitchen table. There were only two chairs. There was no other family and Lorraine rarely had visitors. Josh's random playmates were not allowed inside the house.

"What do you think about Mrs. Lockerbie?"

Joshua looked confused. He scratched his neck.

"She's nice."

Lorraine smirked and pulled from her cigarette. She looked at her son and let out a slow exhale of smoke.

"Really? You think she's nice?" she said, sounding unconvinced. "Boy, you know how I met your daddy?"

"Yes. You said you met him at church."

Lorraine grinned and took another drag.

"That was a lie. I met your daddy at a pool hall. He was fine. Tall. Black as all night. In those days, light skin was the 'in' thing. I guess it still is. But not for me. I liked 'em black. Black and big. The bigger and blacker, the better. You took after me. Yo' daddy was black as tar. You could only see his teeth and his eyes. He was fine, though. Sexy. Charming. Too bad the motherfucka wasn't shit. But you know what? Everybody respected him. Do you want people to respect you?"

Joshua nodded. He looked up at the time on their white microwave. He knew it was late and that he would be exhausted in the morning.

"Yes, ma'am."

"Do you know what *respect* means?"

"Yes."

"What does it mean?"

"It means that people won't try to hurt you or take your stuff."

Lorraine pursed her lips as the smoke fled.

"Is that what it means?"

"Yes."

She flicked her ashes. Her black nightgown hung low onto the floor. Joshua's toes dangled and tapped the kitchen's cold, brown linoleum.

"Your teacher said the best you can hope for is a B-minus. You believe that?"

Joshua looked down at the floor.

"Do you believe that?" Lorraine asked in a louder voice. Joshua looked back up. His mother's round face looked hard behind the smoky haze.

"Yes. The work is hard, Mama. I don't really like school all that much."

"You don't like school?" She glanced at the ashtray. "I can understand that. I can relate. I hated school, too. But see, Joshua, in life, you will have bills to pay. Nothing is free. You want to be like me, a goddamn secretary? Listening to those racist white folks? Taking their goddamn orders like a slave? Is that what you want?"

"No, ma'am."

"Well, don't get your grades together, and that's exactly what's gonna happen to you. Cs ain't good enough, boy. No, sir. Cs won't cut it in the white man's world. Those little white boys sitting next to you in class can goof off and fuck around in class all day and make Cs and Ds and still get a fair shake at life. You know why?"

Joshua scratched his bushy hair, then his back, under the shirt.

"No."

"No? Baby, they can make shitty grades and be okay because they're white. You got that? The system is built to make you fail. Watch you fall like somebody pushed you out a goddamn airplane."

Lorraine stared at her son. She then cleared her throat.

"*Lord, I find it so hard, to live my life, in which I struggle and pray every day,*" she sang with a soulful intensity. "*And in the end, Lord, I will pray, that You will keep me safe, in every way.*"

"Son, always remember, nothing in life lasts forever. This is merely a snapshot."

She mashed the rest of the cigarette in the ashtray.

"It's late. Go to bed."

CHAPTER 5

NOVEMBER 24, 2005
NOON

"Baby? Baby, I think it's time. Josh? Are you there? I think it's time!" Moist beads dotted Kathryn's head. She handed a change of clothes to Roxanne, who had flown to Virginia from California a few days earlier to help out.

"Really? Okay. Okay. I'm on my way. Are you excited? How far apart are the contractions?"

"Close."

"Wow. Are you serious? How close? I'm not far. I'm leaving the Huntington Metro station. How far apart are the contractions?"

"Close! Come on! Get here! Roxanne can drive me, if you can't make it."

"I can make it. I'm turning down Route One now. I'll be there soon."

The autumn days still clung to the summer warmth as Joshua sped home. The leaves had yet to change colors in their apartment complex, so when he finally got home he was greeted by vibrant hues of green and a laboring wife, ready to go at any minute.

"Bags all packed? You have your change of clothes and everything the baby is going to need?"

"Yes, Josh," Roxanne said. "We're good to go."

"Yes, honey." Kathryn appeared nearly out of breath. "It's time. Hope you're ready for this baby."

Joshua smiled and kissed her on the cheek. He gently caressed the back of her neck with his index finger.

"Oh yeah, I'm definitely ready. Definitely. Here, let me get the door."

XXX

"Hello. We're the Lyons."

"Oh. I'm sorry, sir. I didn't see you standing there," the receptionist said, pushing a lock of gray hair behind her ear.

"Hi. We're the Lyons. L-Y-O-N. Doctor Richards is our doctor," Joshua said and then looked around. The hospital staff on the unit was busy bringing new life into the world. Paper-thin scrubs in pink and blue crisscrossed and converged at nursing stations and at the unit secretary's desk. Brown cut-out turkeys with fake yellow, red, and orange feathers hung from a row of cabinets.

"You know, on the way over here, I was thinking about the hospital," Joshua said to Roxanne and Kathryn, who was now seated in a wheelchair practicing her breathing technique. "Do you all realize this is the only time people come to the hospital for happy reasons? Think about it."

Kathryn looked at him and nodded.

"I ain't so sure, Josh," Roxanne said, frowning a bit. "I mean, you could be in here because of one bad decision after the night-club. Too many apple martinis at happy hour could land you in here with a baby."

"Right. Thanks, Roxanne. Well, we're in here for a happy reason. Right, Kat?"

"Yes, honey."

"That's right." Joshua pushed his glasses up on his nose and knelt down and kissed Kathryn on her sweaty forehead. "I love you."

The waiting room was packed with bodies and the scent of medication and cleanser. Bright lights hung above and reflected off the smooth white floors. Multiple languages filled their ears as they waited to be called back.

"Lyons? Joshua and Kathryn?" a young nurse asked, her hair pulled back in a neat ponytail.

"Yes."

"Great. My name is Megan. I'll be your nurse today. Your room is ready. Come back with me."

They walked down the hall, passing anxious dads and wily toddlers trying to get a peek at mommy. An energy of expectation filled the unit.

"How far apart are the contractions?"

"About five minutes," Joshua was quick to answer. "And I think she's in pain."

"Okay. That's normal with her contractions being about five minutes apart," the nurse said, jotting it down in a notebook. "Here's your room 316."

Once inside, Roxanne and Josh began unpacking and preparing Kathryn's things. Having changed into her gown, she climbed into bed and laid her back on a stack of pillows.

"Why do they make these things out of paper? They must want your whole ass to show!"

Joshua and Roxanne laughed. The nurse also smiled as she began hooking Kathryn up to different monitors: one for her and one for the baby. She then pulled a pen from a pocket near her breast.

"Okay. Everything's looking good. The doctor is on his way.

We had to page him but he should be here shortly. Would you like some ice chips?"

"Yes," Kathryn said, timing her response to fit her breathing pattern.

"Okay. Great. I'll be right back. Push this button here, if you need anything. You're in a private room so make yourself at home. The chair in the corner folds out into a sleeper for dad."

"Thank you, Megan." Joshua said. The nurse sauntered out. Joshua smiled. "She was nice. She seems like a good nurse. A little young, but I'm sure she's good."

"I don't know." Roxanne shrugged. "Give me an old nurse. An old black nurse. Fat. One that used to deliver babies in the living room. I need someone with some experience."

"Right, Roxanne." Joshua sat next to Kathryn. "You need a man first. There's only been one virgin birth that I know of. Oh, but you're not a virgin."

"Shut up, Josh. Goofy ass." Roxanne slapped his arm. The slap was more dismissive than playful. "I don't care if you stopped wearing glasses, you still goofy as hell. And you trying to work out now? The gym finally said its trainers needed to look like they're in shape?"

Kathryn chuckled.

"Girl, my man has always looked good." She rubbed Joshua's shoulder.

"Whatever." Roxanne searched through her handbag. "You might need to watch him, Kat. Your hunter-gatherer might be trying to hunt and gather something new. You know what they say about women when they gain that baby weight? It's a turn-off."

"Roxanne, please." Joshua smirked. "Don't get upset because no one is trying to hunt or gather you."

Kathryn chuckled again. "You two are crazy. Acting like you're the married ones."

"Gross." Roxanne inspected Josh from head to toe. "I don't think so, girl. Anyway, I'm going to get some coffee. You guys want anything?"

"No, we're good," Joshua answered, rubbing his bald head.

"Okay."

Joshua unzipped his jacket and hung it on the back of his chair. He stared at his wife. A halogen bulb above them purred like a gleaming cat.

"Babe, you look so beautiful. Are you ready? I'm so excited."

"I'm ready. A little nervous. But I'm ready."

"I understand. I'm a little nervous, too. I love you so much." Joshua grabbed her left hand and caressed it. His fingers ran over the small diamond on her ring finger. "I never thought this would happen for me. I never saw myself with a child. I can't wait to be a father."

Kathryn smiled.

"I know. It's okay. Neither one of us had the best parents. Now it's our turn. I wish my mother was here. I wonder what she would think. Who knows what my father would have thought?"

"Yeah, I thought about that, too. I think my mother would have been surprised, honestly. She liked you. But she probably would have still been shocked. I know your parents are looking down at us now, just like my mom," Joshua paused. "Too bad my dad isn't around. Guess things happen for a reason. Now I can be a good dad."

A nurse came in and checked Kathryn's vitals again. She eyed the two monitors, took some quick notes, and was gone again, her swiftness creating a polite breeze.

"Sometimes I think about the other one," Kathryn said, looking up at the ceiling. "Do you ever think about the other one, Josh?"

Joshua gave his wife an intense gaze. He looked down at the mattress, then the floor. Outside the room, a child could be heard running and laughing, his chasing father in hot pursuit.

"I love you so much, Kathryn. We did what we had to do at the time. Okay? This is our chance, now, to be parents, to be great parents. The kind we always wanted."

"Damn kids are going to drive me crazy," Roxanne said, walking through the doorway sipping a cup of hot coffee. The bitterness made her lips purse. "Patrice called. She and Dawn are on their way. She sounded really excited."

"Did she?" Kathryn smiled. Joshua stood up. "That's good."

"I know. I haven't seen Dawn since she was a baby. She's probably getting big."

Joshua frowned at Roxanne and kneeled back down to Kathryn's side and caressed her forehead. Her light-brown hair had grown tremendously during the pregnancy, and it cascaded down the side of the pillow like a waterfall.

"We've been through a lot, honey. Terrorist attacks. Hurricane Isabel. You remember that?"

"How could I forget?" Kathryn smiled. "I'd never seen wind blow trees sideways for so long. Just give me an earthquake or a mudslide...maybe even a forest fire. I can't deal with hurricanes."

"I know. I'd rather take a tornado any day. Heck, give me an ice storm." Joshua laughed. "And remember the sniper? You were scared as hell. You remember that?"

"Shit, Josh. Don't make my heart rate go through the damn roof. *Everybody* was scared. I couldn't put gas in the car without nearly peeing on myself. Had me looking for white box trucks. That shit was terrifying. Some damn crazy-ass brothas. Everybody just *knew* it was some deranged, ex-military white guy from Iowa or something. That was crazy."

"Yeah. It was. But we made it. We made it. I'm so excited, babe. This is it. We're about to have a baby. This is the happiest day of my life."

Kathryn winced. Joshua quickly took her hand.

"I'm fine," she said.

"Okay."

Joshua looked up at the television mounted to the wall and saw that his favorite movie was on. He grinned widely.

"Oh no, not *Known Teeth Kingz*," Kathryn said with a frown as another contraction kicked in. Joshua motioned to her to be quiet as he turned the volume up.

"Fucking right, we're going to win, J-Rod. Sanchez. Ain't that right, Nguyen?"

Nguyen went back to wiping his helmet. A dry gale traipsed across the sandy plateau.

"I'm just saying, we've been in this shithole country for five months." Sanchez flicked an insect from his neck.

"Well, don't you worry about that, Sanny ole boy. You see that over there?" Jackson pointed to the snowcapped peaks in the distance. "That's home, baby. That's what we came for. Almost there now, Sanny ole boy. Almost there."

"Yeah, I know. But fuck, did all those fucking villagers have to die? I mean, they were probably going to die in the next few weeks, but—"

"But nothin', Sanny. Fuck them goddamn chinks. Like I said, we did them fucks a favor. You've seen how those fuckers look when they go from the dry. The dry is a horrible fucking way to go. We ending

their miserable lives with honor. It's a goddamn honor to meet God with a Marine round in your fucking head."

"Ain't that the truth." Rodriguez knocked off the rest of his water and tossed the plastic cube to the sand. "We're Americans, Sanny. You know how we do it. We don't ask nobody for shit. We take it."

"You goddamn right. Tell your boy, J-Rod." Jackson leaned forward and the rage in his eyes smoldered by the camp light.

"If those fucking chinks didn't walk out on us and the rest of the fucking world at the International Water Summit, we wouldn't be here putting American boots up their asses!"

"Amen to that." Rodriguez smirked. Jackson again reclined in his tent.

"I know about the goddamn summit, asshole. Okay? I don't need a fucking history lesson." Sanchez was now leaning toward Rodriguez. Nguyen and Jackson seemed uninterested. "All I'm saying is that we could have been more diplomatic. We could have tried to bring them back to the table."

"Please. Don't kid yourself," Rodriguez said. "They saw what we did in Eastern Europe, in Central Africa. We don't negotiate. We decapitate."

Sanchez waved a lazy hand at Rodriguez as if shooing another annoying insect.

"Look, fuck face, you want to sit around and negotiate while your mother and sister are dying from the dry? You want to sit around while their fucking eyeballs sink into their skulls and mangy dogs gnaw at them while they're still alive? In case you didn't know it, asshole, we're at war."

"Yeah, a war we started."

"Wise the fuck up! The freshening don't give a fuck what flag you fly. We're all dead meat, eventually." Rodriguez slapped Sanchez's boot and stormed off to another group that was playing dominos a few meters away.

"The freshening." Sanchez sighed.

"That's right, fuck boy. Good ole global warming." Jackson propped his elbow up and rested his weight on it. "Those goddamn polar caps melted and blam*! Too much fresh water in the ocean."*

Nguyen placed his helmet in the tent and sat out in the sand listening to Jackson.

"Those suits knew it was coming." Jackson laughed. "Now we're all meteorology scientists in this bitch. Too much fresh in salt means flooded coasts, monster hurricanes, and baby hallelujah, send in the Marines!"

"And so now it's China's turn to burn?"

"You goddamn right. Those dumb fucks agreed to dump their nukes. So now it's time for an old-fashioned, Marine ass-kickin'. We meet up with Delta Company at the Szinwuan Pass one hundred kilometers from here and it's half a day's hump up to the base of the Himalayas. After that, it's General Kwinluan's last stand. He better bring all he's got, because Mama Marine wants her fresh motherfuckin' water. His ass is going to fall like those fucks at Kilamanjaro, and those weak fucks in the Alps. We kick ass and take names."

Rodriguez returned to this hutch just as fast as he had left it (that quickly he had lost two weeks' pay playing mahjong). Deflated, he cracked open an old book—an ancient tale of war and strategy and of life. He had heard it was a tale chock full of uplifting shit. He needed that. He picked up where he had left off.

"I just wish there was another way." Sanchez kicked a pebble with his boot and stared at his rifle, dusty and yet to be cleaned.

"Please. No venga with that bullshit. When we get to the top of that peak, I'm goin' to mash my boot in Kwinluan's ass and crush that snow in my hand and take a long, long drink."

Joshua looked back at Kathryn and smiled.

"We're having a baby. Happiest day of my life."

CHAPTER 6

SEPTEMBER 11, 2001
7:45 A.M.

She nearly missed her train. The shuttle bus from her apartment complex was late picking up the riders, so she was forced to run for her Yellow Line train at the Huntington Metro station.

"Trice, girl, I'm running late." She quickly checked the time on her cell phone. "Yeah, sis. It's here. Okay. Let me call you back. I'll see you tonight. Bye."

The train was crowded, but there were still seats available. If Kathryn had a choice, she preferred a row to herself. If the train was full, her preference would be a seat at least facing forward. She hated to sit with her back toward the front, and today she was, although she sat next to the window.

The train exited the station. The sun was up now. Not a cloud in the sky. This section of the line was above ground, before it sank into the earth and the darkened tunnels, and the sun was beautifully warm. Kathryn opened a book and began to read. It was her daily routine as she rode to her job at the Pentagon.

This was a new book. She flipped through the pages, a piece someone at worked had loaned her.

A drive through the countryside can be relaxing. Sometimes you don't see a soul for miles, allowing for deep contemplation or just the opposite: no thoughts at all. But I guess if you're not used to that it can be a little unsettling. Growing up in a place surrounded by numerous structures and vertical forms does offer a sense of protection, if at the least, from the forces of nature. But every so often in the rural lands, in between the fields of waist-high golden reeds, interjecting into the wide tranquility of a picture-perfect baby-blue sky, there can be a conspicuous and welcomed sign of life.

Around her men in suits and women in skirts and blazers read their newspapers, listened to music, or stared off into space, likely dreading the tasks that awaited them. She read more.

Sometimes, her grandeur juts out of the ground into the air over fifty feet. She's bedecked in the color of a Catholic cardinal's biretta, or that of a waning rose whose fragrance has pleased to the fullest extent; having served its purpose it can simply do no more. She is trimmed in what resembles the brilliant gleam of a south Pacific pearl, crafted by similar fashions that require care and diligence. Her heart is a huge doorway, permitting the passage of tenderness.

Kathryn suddenly heard a loud rustling. She looked up from the book to her left.

A woman with long blond hair sat with one leg in a cast, propped up on her briefcase. She had on jeans, a navy-blue blazer, and a turquoise shirt. Kathryn thought the turquoise was nice. The woman sat next to a man who was reading a newspaper. He opened it to read an inside story. Kathryn could tell the jostling angered the woman. The man's hand and elbow were nearly touching her. The blonde leaned away, first giving him a look of irritation. She reached for the newsletter she had tucked under her right arm. It left white specks on her blazer.

The train cruised into the next station. Riders got on and off.

There was a mostly silent shifting of bodies and positions. Oxfords and flats, pumps and boots and trainers politely found their way. The train left the station. Kathryn nestled into a comfortable place. She had ridden the train for sometime now, but every day was different. Delays. Power outages. A sick passenger vomiting. Stations being closed. A depressed bean counter jumping on the tracks.

The train arrived at the next station. People got off and others got on. Someone inadvertently brushed against the blond woman's briefcase. It fell and a current of pain shot from her foot up her spine. She winced. The man next to her turned the page of his paper. It was loud and sweeping. The train slowly left the station. The woman painfully leaned over to prop her suitcase back up. She gingerly remounted her foot and slowly leaned back into her seat. The man shook his paper. She frowned. He shook his paper again. She shook her head and opened her newsletter. He shook his paper again. She frowned, this time more dramatically. He seemed to edge closer to her. Her jaw tightened. He shook his paper again.

"Excuse me, sir. I don't have a lot of room here. As you can see, my leg is in a cast."

The man looked up from his paper and stared at the woman. Then he took a nonchalant glance at her leg, cast resting on her briefcase.

"If my paper is bothering you, by all means, call the *Washington Post.*"

"Excuse me?"

"I said call the *Post*. Or, you can move. Heck, you have one good leg, stand on it."

"You want me to stand? With a broken leg? What kind of asshole are you?" the woman screamed. She swiped at his paper. The commotion filled the train.

"I beg your pardon, miss! Don't touch my paper. Don't ever touch my paper! Like I said, if you don't like it, by all means, move! I was in the seat first, okay? Get up, if you don't like it!"

The woman stared at the man.

"Fine!" She grabbed her briefcase, hobbled across the aisle to the seat next to Kathryn, and sat down.

"Fucking asshole," she said, loud enough for him and others to hear. Kathryn slid her butt away from the woman, wanting to give her as much room as possible. Kathryn hated the feeling of a stranger's body touching her. She had lost her page in the book. She fanned throughout until she found it.

She is staunch but doting. Built firmly to withstand the strongest storm but sheltering enough to accommodate the softest down. Inside you might find enthusiastic youth zealous at existence and prancing about to prove it. Or you may come across aged wisdom that has seen and done it all, now satisfied to simply enjoy the gentle breeze and the bounty of the earth, taking the wondrous star-filled night for granted.

There are chambers inside that each hold something special. Sectioned off and protected, the things that dwell here know they are cherished. At her apex, where beds of bronze silky hairs lay, is often where dreams are hatched and wishes realized. Yes, her presence in the countryside can be reassuring.

Unfortunately, we haven't been to the countryside in quite some time. And this great form that I'm thinking of that juts into the big beautiful blue will one day no longer contain youthful zeal. The pearly gleam will one day be more of an ecru, a worn egg-shell type of hue. The deep crimson that once encircled her will be faded by burdens and time. She will be more the tone of fresh clay, much like soil that no longer yields ripe fruit. Her gated heart will be imperfectly slanted, cracked and splintered. Her strong facade will be leaning remnants of inert pine with huge cavities and wide gaps. One day she will represent the last of her kind. This amazing form may one day be surrounded by new luster and new elements that tower above her. Do not fear it. It is the natural order of things.

And yet, the youth that once lived there will grow to be wise. The contents she once cherished will be cherished by the world. The stars that lovingly winked at her will wink at us! Her crimson coat will exist more gloriously in the hearts and minds of those who loved her than it ever did in life. Hold fast to the comfort and protection she provided when the rain was falling and the hail was crashing.

Yes. Some day from now, the time for cranberry-colored sanctuaries with floors of satiny hair the color of sunshine will pass. She can do no more. It will be up to those whom she touched, to savor her sweet memory. This they must do, to the fullest extent.

The train arrived at the Pentagon. Kathryn packed away her book and prepared to exit. She grabbed her purse and stood by the door. She looked back at the man with the paper and the woman with the cast. They were again in their own worlds, once again indifferent to each other.

XXX

Even though she had been working at the Pentagon for over a year, the sight of men and women in uniform still intrigued her. In a way it made her feel special—like she was part of an exclusive club. After all, not everyone could work at the Pentagon. The interview process was extensive, and took weeks. She and Josh were looking for jobs and they were getting low on funds. She saw the opening in the paper and jumped at it. How many of her friends in California could say they worked at the Pentagon? Not one. Roxanne had applied for a job there. Unfortunately, a little run-in with the law in junior high school ended her chances.

"Goddamn it! Where's the creamer?" Charlene yelled to the other secretaries in the break room. "See, one of those fat bitches has taken the goddamn creamer to their desk. What the hell are they using it for? Snorting it like coke?"

Kathryn laughed. She saw Charlene as the little sister she never had. Every morning she and Charlene would prepare their coffee together. They sat on opposite sides of the office, and once the workday got underway, they rarely saw each other until lunchtime or after work.

"Girl, I don't know. There should be some creamer in the cabinet above the sink. That's the secret stash."

Charlene smiled and checked the cabinet.

"Yes! I can finally start my day. I can't handle these D.O.D. jerks without my morning Joe."

They walked out the break room toward their desks, passing their supervisor Demetria on the way.

"Ladies."

"Hey, Demetria," Kathryn said.

"Oh my God, did you all see this?" Demetria asked, looking at the small break-room television.

Charlene kept walking but Kathryn stopped and looked back.

"What?"

"A plane just flew into the World Trade Center in New York. Looks like an accident. That's sad."

"Oh my goodness, that is sad." Kathryn walked back toward

the break room. Her fingertips gently spun the maroon stick in her coffee. "Did the pilot go off course?"

"I guess he had to," Demetria said, preparing a cup of coffee while keeping her eyes on the television. "I'm sure a lot of people were in the building. That's just so sad."

Kathryn shook her head in disbelief, then headed back to her desk. She had some paperwork to go over. It was due at ten and she still had a few edits to make. A date was wrong. Someone had told her the wrong room number so that had to be changed, too. She took a sip of coffee. She flinched. The hot liquid burned her tongue. She flipped the light switch over her desk. The bulb flickered several times, then fully illuminated the paperclips, and ink pens scattered about. She logged onto her computer. *Access denied*, the screen read. She tried again, this time entering her user name and password more slowly. *Access denied.*

"Damn it."

She looked on her board and found the number for I.T. She picked up the phone.

"Welcome to the I.T. Help Desk. Please enter your employee number," the recording chirped.

"Damn it! I don't know my employee number," Kathryn mumbled to herself. She opened a desk drawer and fumbled through it looking for the slip with her employee number. Her fingers rambled over a pack of Ramen Noodles. A comb. A picture of Joshua. A compact mirror. She finally found it and punched in the numbers.

"Thank you, Kathryn Lyon. Your wait time is approximately five minutes. Please hold."

Kathryn let out a deep exhale.

"Great way to start a damn morning. Fucking Defense Department," she grumbled. She sat there several minutes, listening to static air. No voice. No music. Just still air. She fingered a paper clip. She looked out over her cubicle wall. She could see several more people staring at the TV in the break room. Their bodies were stiff. Their faces were blank. Some were talking. She couldn't make out what they saying. She took the phone away from her ear and stood up. A hush came over the normally loud corridor. There was silence.

"What's going on?"

Demetria turned toward her. Her eyes were wide. Her voice was calm.

"Oh my God, Kathryn. A second plane has hit the World Trade Center. That can't be an accident. Two planes? It can't be."

The phone on Demetria's desk suddenly rang.

Kathryn stood with the phone in hand.

Someone picked up. "I.T. This is Bill. How can I help?"

"Hey, Bill." Kathryn sank back into her seat. "I'm having… I'm having some trouble logging in."

"No problem," Bill said. "I can easily access your computer and reset the password. How's that sound?"

Demetria suddenly slammed her phone down.

"We all have to get out! Now! A hijacked airplane is headed this direction!"

"Kathryn? Are you there?" Bill asked. A second line on his end began to ring.

Kathryn froze. "What? What did you say, Demetria?"

"I said get out! We have to go. Get off the phone. Everybody, listen up. We're going to exit out the Corridor C exit. Okay?" She turned to Kathryn. "Kat, let's go, now."

Kathryn looked at the phone. "Bill, I think you should get out," she whispered. She then slowly lowered the phone back to the base and hung up. Then they heard it.

An explosion rocked the building and echoed throughout the corridors. The force knocked two silver paperclips off Kathryn's desk. Dreadful vibrations shot through the floor through her body into her heart. Kathryn reached for her cell phone.

"Run!"

She ran as fast as she could. Hundreds flooded the corridors. Her heart was pumping fast. On both sides she was flanked by the terrified. Their rank was insignificant. The bars on their white and tan uniforms were hidden by the wild flailing of arms and the gray blur of bodies. No one noticed who brushed past them. No one paid attention to who was crying next to them. Who they were as individuals was not important. They had been attacked. Kathryn felt as if she was running in slow motion. No matter how much her heart and her lungs ached, she wasn't moving fast enough. She couldn't move fast enough. It was like a dream. She wanted to stop and look back. She could feel the rush of humanity, like a stampede, chasing behind. Tears stained her face. Thoughts ran through her head. *Joshua. Patrice. Daddy. All those people. Am I going to die? I'm going to die! All those people. Kids? Did kids die? Oh my God. Dear, God! Why, God? Why is this happening? It's the end of world. It has to be. It's happening. It's now. Joshua. Those kids. Those babies. Why, God?*

She wanted to faint. She wanted to stop running. It was a terrible dream. She wanted to look back. But she couldn't. She was afraid. She ran as fast as she could. They were passing her on both sides now, men and women in uniform. She felt like they were leaving her. She couldn't keep up. She grew even more frightened. The building would collapse upon her, she thought, trapping her forever. They would have to use the dogs to find her body. Camouflage fatigues and flight suits became a jumble. Everyone was terrified. She could see it in their eyes. She was afraid. They could all smell the smoke.

"Oh my God! Baby, are you okay?" Joshua panted heavily into the phone. Just outside the office, panicked workers ran out or called friends and family members on their cell phones.

"Oh, Josh, honey. Yes, I'm okay." Kathryn looked around the parking lot. Men and woman of all races were scrambling searching for friends and coworkers. Many wore military garb, some had on civilian clothes. Firefighters arrived on the scene, scrambling to unravel hoses and douse the flames that were consuming a portion of the huge fortress.

"Oh, honey, it's so good to hear your voice. I've been calling you for like ten minutes. I can see the smoke from the gym. I didn't think you were on that side, but I wasn't sure."

"Oh God, Josh. So many people have been hurt. Were we bombed? Somebody said they drove a truck up to the Pentagon and bombed us. Who would do that?"

She looked around again. Military Police and persons with medical training ran toward the smoke and the debris. Helicopters from nearby hospitals flew and searched for landing areas, their blades chopping the smoky air. Pulverized rock and dust elements rained down. She cleared her sandy throat. A beautiful day everywhere else was a blackened sky that rained ash where she stood. Paper and debris fluttered.

"Okay, honey. You have to get out of there. It wasn't a bomb. They're saying it was a terrorist attack. Two planes flew into the Twin Towers in New York." Joshua was silent for a moment.

He could hear Kathryn crying on the other end. "Look, I'm on my way to get you. I'm leaving here now."

"Oh my God, honey. What if it's not over? What if they try to bomb the White House? Or someplace else?"

"Look, Kathryn. I'm coming to get you. Okay?"

"But I took the train. I don't think they'll let me down there. This is so crazy, Josh. The whole side of the Pentagon is on fire. People are running around all over the place, bleeding, screaming. I can't find Demetria or Charlene."

"Then walk. I don't care. I'll walk to you. Okay? You can't worry about your supervisor right now. And I'm sure Charlene is okay. She knows how to take care of herself."

"But Charlene's my friend. What if she's hurt?" Kathryn wildly looked around the parking lot and began calling out for her friend.

"Honey, Kathryn. It will be okay. I'm sure they're fine. I'm on my way. I love you."

Kathryn dropped to her knees and the hard pavement scratched through her pantyhose, causing her knees to bleed in thin slivers. Cars burned in an adjacent parking lot, sparked by the flames of the explosion. Kathryn saw a long line form for the pay phone. Hundreds stood anxiously waiting for their turn to call loved ones. Bloody bodies lay in the grass.

"Okay. Okay. Okay, Josh..." Her voice was faint as a whisper. "I love you so much."

"I love you, too, baby. You know the road to Columbia Pike? Near the underpass?"

"Yes."

"Okay. Good. I'm walking that way. You start walking, too. Okay?"

"Hello? Josh? You're breaking up. What did you say?"

"Kathryn? Do you hear me? I said, the underpass by Columbia Pike. Are you there?"

"Joshua? Josh? I can't hear you."

XXX

Joshua gazed out the window and saw only the top of the Pentagon and a wide plume of black smoke. He slammed the phone down and bolted toward the door.

"Dude, where are you going? This shit might not be over," said Sean, a trainer at the sports club.

"Man, that's my wife," Joshua said, feeling the emotion in his voice.

"Those military guys won't let you over there!"

Joshua checked his pants for his wallet and keys. On the floor, terrified gym clients sobbed and dialed numbers on cell phones, while others bolted through the doors, leaving everything they brought behind them. Joshua turned for the door, then glanced back at Sean.

"That's my wife. I'm going to get her."

And there he was. Running down the highway. The beautiful sky above betrayed by sorrowful motes that ascending heavenward. He ran past a designer shoe store and its supple Italian leather. He ran past a coffee shop with its Spanish sizes. He ran as fast as he could, passing the foreign furniture maker and the organic grocery store; all the while the black grew larger and larger in the cloudless sky. Sweat, fear, anxiety and pain left his body.

Joshua was soaked and foul by the time he reached the outer

perimeter of the Pentagon, the police blockade, and the horde of rescue workers. Military personnel and other people were still fleeing.

"Sir! Please, you have to stand back. This area is a secure location."

"My. My. My wife," he gasped. "My wife works here. Kathryn. Kathryn Lyon."

"Sir. Calm down. We are still assessing the situation. Do you know where your wife is?"

Joshua removed his glasses, dropped to his knees and struggled not to sob.

"No. I spoke to her. I think she's okay. But...but I don't know." He covered his face with his hand. "Why did this have to happen? I just. I just don't understand."

"Joshua!" It was a distant wail. Like a phantom wind traipsing through maple leaves. He thought he heard it. His heart skipped, but he wasn't sure.

"Joshua! Here I am. Oh, honey. You found me." Kathryn's face was stained with mascara streaks. Her white blouse was speckled with soot. "Baby, I'm okay."

Joshua peeled himself from the hard asphalt. He embraced her. "I know. I know you told me you were okay," he said, trying to again speak in his normal deep voice. He wiped his face and put his glasses back on. "But I didn't see you. Then the guard wouldn't let me in. I got scared. Baby, I'm so glad you're okay. Let's get out of here.

"But how? The train is shut down."

"It doesn't matter. We'll walk. Look."

Kathryn looked up the road and saw hundreds, maybe thousands, of people walking. They were headed in all directions.

"Come on. We can walk, too. Let's go home."

They walked and walked. For hours. Kathryn recognized a few guys from the Pentagon's barbershop and some from the credit union, so they all walked together, south toward Alexandria.

"My boss was still in there," one said.

"I wonder if we're going to war?" another questioned.

"How many people were on those planes, and in the World Trade Center? Why would they attack us like that? Are we going to get hit again?" The questions came in flurries.

***

It was nightfall when Joshua and Kathryn walked into their apartment building. It took them ten hours to walk home. Kathryn held her pumps in her hand. The bottom of her feet were bloodied and blistered. Joshua had held her other hand the entire time. They looked at each other and smiled. They had survived. They were alive. Joshua pushed the metal arrow and called for the elevator. He stared at Kathryn. They didn't exchange any words. They simply stood there, and waited for the elevator to whisk them away.

CHAPTER 7

JUNE 30, 2008
7:13 P.M.

They were excited when they found the small, two-bedroom apartment. Little Josh was getting bigger, and the one-bedroom place they had would no longer hold their possessions. The novelty of having a small child in the middle of the bed had worn off. Kathryn and Joshua needed their space, so the two-bedroom in Del Ray seemed like a blessing.

Five short stairs down inside the building's secure door led to the hallway where their basement apartment was located. To the left, their neighbors from Arkansas; to the right, the Lyon place. Joshua always had to duck his head when he went down the stairs. At night it was poorly lit, and if he went out with Chidu for drinks, he occasionally forgot to duck. The brick impact against his bald head served as an unwelcome reminder.

Just inside the door one could see their entire apartment. Straight ahead was the sofa they had gotten from Kathryn's father about a month before he died. Later they would think he knew he was dying, which is why he began giving things away. It was her idea to place a slipcover over the old velvet flower pattern. To the right was the wicker-based dining room table with the glass top her father also had given them. The wicker chairs were covered in a soft burgundy cotton from the back to the floor—again her idea. The window was at head height, the apartment being in the basement. On sunny days, the small residence would be flush with bright light. On cloudy days, a sullen fog enveloped the young family and made it hard to rise in the morning.

Their walls were mostly bare. In a short hall, which was not much of a hall—perhaps only two of Joshua's long strides—hung a photo of him and his bride. Not on their wedding day. No one was at their wedding but them and the Justice of the Peace who married them. They laughed because he spoke with an exaggerated Texas twang. It was an inside joke that they enjoyed immensely. No, the photo that hung in the short non-hallway was one taken of them the week they moved to Virginia. Technically, they were staying at Ledroit's home in Prince George's County, Maryland. He fancied himself a photographer, taking random shots at the dinner table, while watching the game or washing the car. Ledroit took this snapshot, so the Lyons saw it fitting to hang it in their home; a sign of reverence and remembrance.

Their bedroom was bare. No painting graced the walls; no color at all could be seen. They had a frame, a box spring, a mattress and two flimsy pillows. They kept their clothes neatly hung in the double closet, the one high point of the apartment. Little Josh's room actually had more space, so Kathryn would sneak a few of her belongings in there. A skirt or dress for work, maybe a few pair of boots that were out of season. His crib and toys occupied the other space. Trucks and bears and balls littered the room. When they took a tour of the place, Joshua proudly envisioned himself painting the room blue, embellishing it with baseballs, basketballs and footballs. Months later, the walls were still eggshell white.

A large gray television sat directly in front of the covered sofa. The TV stand was rickety—during the move Joshua lost two screws that held it in place. The intimacy of the room made it so only one person could pass by at a time. The close quarters would often seem to suffocate them. Joshua seemed most affected by it. That was a few months ago.

"It was something me and Chidu talked about. You don't want to travel and go to new places?"

Kathryn shook her head. "I'm happy here. We have everything we need. Our family. A roof over our heads. Food on the table. Plus, that means we would have to get on a plane. No way that's happening."

"We?" Joshua looked up from his plate.

Kathryn giggled.

"You think you're traveling to Africa by yourself? Ha! That ain't happening. And I'm not going, so that means you're not going. How about we all drive up to New York, or Atlantic City?"

Joshua frowned. He looked back down at his plate.

"Kathryn, can you please tell me why this food is so bland? What? They don't make seasoning anymore? Just because you don't eat, doesn't mean I have to suffer."

"I ate, Josh." Her voice quickly became low and contrite. "What's up with the attitude all of a sudden?"

"I'm fine. I can't believe you ate. A word for the wise—that skinny stuff ain't sexy."

She didn't reply. She continued to wipe and store the pots and pans used to make the dinner.

Joshua undid a button on his shirt. He sighed again. The wicker table wobbled.

"You know, Kat, I bust my ass all day at that gym. Dealing with jerks, trying to help these fat, lazy people lose weight. All

I ask for is a fucking decent meal when I get home. Is that too much to ask? You don't even have a fucking job. I mean, what's your excuse?"

Tension rolled up into her shoulders. She slowly exhaled.

"Why are you cursing? What has gotten into you? Do you have to talk like that? In front of Josh junior?" Soap suds from the sponge she was using bubbled on the stovetop in thousands of sweet-smelling circles.

"Daddy, no," the little boy said.

Joshua glanced over at his son, his caramel skin lit by the light of the kitchen. The boy smiled at him and separated his noodles one by one, then slurped them individually.

"I don't get it, Kat. What did you put on these pork chops? They taste like old Timberlands."

The baby laughed.

"Timbermans." The child giggled.

Kathryn placed a large pot in the cabinet above the stove. Her sleek black pants showed her body's thinness.

"Remember last time you were at the grocery store?" She didn't look at him. "I asked you to bring home some black pepper and seasoning salt because we ran out."

"So if something runs out, I have to go get it? Why couldn't you go get it?"

Joshua shoved the plate away. Little Josh slapped at the white plastic table on his highchair.

"Ready to get down," he sang.

He watched his father closely as he got up from the table and grabbed a beer from the refrigerator. He was standing next to Kathryn as she continued to clean the kitchen.

"Excuse me," she said, using her hip to nudge him away. "Josh, stop messing around, these knives are sharp." She lowered her voice. "They're the only good thing we own."

Joshua used the opener on his key chain to remove the cap from the bottle.

"Excuse me, Joshua! I need to put this food away! "

He took half a step away from the fridge, leaving his wife barely enough space to squeeze by.

"Jerk," she mumbled under her breath.

"What? What did you just say?!" She frowned, then coughed. Her throat was sore.

"Nothing. Excuse me. I can't open the door all the way."

"Forget that door. You know, I don't think I like the way you're talking to me."

Kathryn paused and looked at him.

"Well, you are standing in my way, dear. You see I'm trying to put the leftovers away."

Joshua took a sip of his beer.

"You need to throw this crap away. It's disgusting. I bet you couldn't give this crap to a stray dog."

"Crap," the baby repeated. "Ready to get down now." He swung his chubby arms. He smiled and his dimples deepened. An uneasy feeling suddenly struck Kathryn. She turned around and looked at her husband.

"You know, Josh. You don't have to eat it. You know that? In fact, you don't have to ever worry about eating anything I cook. I'll only cook for myself and the baby from here on out. How does that sound? Would that work for you?"

He took another swig of beer. "Hey, that's cool. Cool for me. I feel sorry for the baby, though."

"Whatever, Joshua. I'm going to put these things away, then

watch my show. You were late so I already missed half of it. You need to buy me a Tivo."

"Your show? Tivo? Please. I don't understand how you can watch that garbage. It's so fake."

"Don't worry about it. You like to watch that one dumb movie every time it comes on, right? So let me have my escape."

"Yeah, okay. *Known Teeth Kingz* is a great movie about the ramifications of global warming. Not to mention they kick a lot of butt."

"Right, Josh."

"Ready to get down," the child said, sounding less happy.

Joshua finished off the rest of the beer and burped loudly.

Kathryn frowned. Little Josh laughed. The sweet chuckle made his father smile.

"You like that, son?"

The boy again laughed; the sound of a tiny angel. It softened Joshua. He walked over to his son, who was covered in spaghetti sauce and noodle bits.

"How was my little man today? Did you miss Daddy?" The boy smiled widely and giggled, throwing a soggy noodle at his father. It stuck to his face.

"Oh! You got me!"

"Got you!"

Joshua yanked his son from his highchair, went into the living room area, and rolled around on the floor with him. They laughed uncontrollably.

"You want to hit Daddy with noodles? Why do you want to hit Daddy with noodles?" He tickled him and the baby laughed.

They giggled and laughed and rolled about the floor. The child's yellow onesie was covered with sauce and now stray balls of lint. When they finally stopped laughing and wrestling, Kathryn had already left the room and started preparing for bed.

"Okay, junior. I guess we should get ready for bed, too. What do you think?"

"No."

The little boy smiled and giggled. He had big, springy, sandy-brown hair. Kathryn's was the same when she was that age.

"You're not ready for your bath?" Joshua asked.

"No bath."

The little boy's voice was high and sweet. Oval dimples pressed into his fat cheeks.

"That's okay. Come on, little guy. You don't have to take a bath. Baths are for girls. Let's get ready for bed."

Joshua carried the little boy in his left arm and kissed him on the cheek before disappearing into the child's room to ready him for bed.

Kathryn laid the hand towel near the sink and sat down in front of the television. For over six years, every Monday, she hadn't missed an episode of her favorite television program: *Devin Gentle*. She smiled as her main character entered the room.

"When someone asks me what line of work I'm in, I become embarrassed, my cheeks flush with rose. This is who I become, even though I'm typically known as a man of poise.

It usually occurs in one of those snooty social settings, like the one tonight, where So and So discusses Mr. Such and Such and his proposal that will do This and That. It's an evening event in which the celestial bodies twinkle outside and distilled water ice chunks swish and shimmy inside silver-bulletlike canisters filled with Grey Goose. The great slate orb nonchalantly hangs in the black sky.

It is at these amorphous shindigs that some elderly debutante, smelling of sweet lily and sandalwood—Elizabeth Taylor's White Diamonds, perhaps—discreetly stumbles over and introduces herself hand first. I've found that it is usually the left hand, since that is the resting place of enormous rocks no doubt given by deceased tycoon husbands. I imagine she calls herself Duchess or Countess.

"My name is Countess, charmed," she says. I respond with my hand and name, barely restraining my laughter. Devin Gentle. Romance novelist, private investigator.

The adjacent rooms, beautifully decorated with abstract artwork painted with vibrant swaths of lavender and peach, are alive with conversation. A bright orange fire crackles in the corner near the fortieth-floor balcony. I blankly stare past the Lalique chandelier out the large sliding glass window at the rows of skyscrapers that seem to go on forever as she chats about Dante and Tolstoy. It seems so pretentious. She effortlessly peppers her sentences with "darling" and "absolutely," stressing the "lute."

I nod as if in total agreement, feeling betrayed by my tailored suit and gold cufflinks on this enigmatic night. I glance about the room. It's an eclectic bunch of tan skin and dyed hair, Botox and unusual accents. Two women and a man converse while comfortably seated on a fine sofa the same color as my dirty martini. It makes me take a wanting look at my drink. This mixture was often the beverage of choice at my Vermont log cabin, once a troubling chapter had been completed or a lengthy tome put to bed. I would also drink it after cracking a troublesome case. The Victoria Heights affair comes to mind. Now the delicious bite of olive juice and vodka seems to mock me. The nostalgia being crushed by this haughty mistress.

"Yes, Dante, great writer," I reply after taking a much-needed swig. "Could you excuse me for a moment? Thank you. It's been a pleasure."

I scurry off like a woodland creature, having barely escaped the hungry jaws of a mountain lion. I make a dash straight to the mahogany bar at the other end of the vast living space. My mocha loafers delicately tap the glossy parquet floors.

"Kathryn."

She angrily turned to Joshua.

"Yes? You see I'm watching my show."

"I know. You can watch it later. Come to bed with me."

"What? No. Let me finish watching my show."

Joshua went into their bedroom and prepared himself for a shower. Kathryn turned back to her program.

The voiceover came and announced that tonight's show would be continued. Kathryn groaned. She turned the television off.

⁂

Joshua and Kathryn both showered. He got into bed with what he usually wore: old gray gym shorts and a tattered gray T-shirt. She came out the shower smelling like the kiwi and mango body cream Josh had bought her for Mother's Day. Her thighs, now more trim, were shiny when the moon snuck in through the blinds and showcased them. Joshua watched as his wife came into the bedroom and closed the door behind her.

"Dang, honey. You're looking pretty sexy," Joshua said. He reached for her shoulder but she pulled away.

"Damn, Kathryn, it's like that?"

"Joshua. The way you talked to me in the kitchen? Is that supposed to be a turn-on?"

He placed his arm back at his side.

"I'm sorry. Look. I'm just…a little tired, and stressed out.

I'm getting tired of this job. It's…it's been a while since we've done anything. You never want to have sex. You act like it's not good anymore."

Kathryn crawled into her side of the bed and placed the comforter over her waist. Her nipples poked through her thin tank top.

"Come on, honey. I'm horny."

"I'm tired, Joshua."

"Come on, Kat." He pulled the blanket down and unveiled himself.

Kathryn sighed.

"I don't feel like having sex tonight." She raised her voice. Joshua smiled at her while he stroked himself. "I'll suck it. But no sex. I'm exhausted."

Joshua agreed and Kathryn lowered her head under the comforter. He felt lightheaded as she pleasured him with her mouth. He pushed her head forcefully. She took it. Within minutes, he came and was fast asleep. Kathryn wiped her mouth with a towel near the nightstand and closed her eyes. She watched Joshua and made sure he was sleeping comfortably.

XXX

When they were both asleep is when she usually did it. She would step lightly, tiptoeing, toward her and Joshua's room. After the first several nights, she learned how far she could open the bedroom door before it creaked. She would peek in, carefully, stopping just shy of the wooden screech. When Joshua's glasses were on the nightstand, and his right arm was over his face, his long dark legs out from under the comforter, he was asleep. She would then check little Josh's room, once more.

The last thing she wanted in life was for the baby to stumble upon her, in a sleep state, rubbing his eyes, confused and scared by what Mommy was doing.

She went into the bathroom and locked the door. She grabbed the plunger, and slowly knelt down in front of the toilet. She lifted the lid. She put the plunger handle near her lips. She leaned over the bowl. A wave rippled. She opened her mouth. She was careful not to hit a tooth. She loved her teeth. Joshua did, too. She edged closer to the bowl. She slid the long handle to the back of her throat.

CHAPTER 8

JANUARY 27, 1997
10:58 P.M.

The District's architecture still fascinated him. He'd never seen anything like it, not in the Midwest. It reminded him of photographs he had seen of England, or was it Norway? Houses smashed together like sand castles, separated by colors or a different sized brick. What was a rowhouse, anyway?

Tonight bass rocked the inside of one of these rowhouses. The students danced, drank Alize and Hennessy, and bobbed their heads.

The rest of the street was quiet. Most of the streetlights were out; either from neglect or from the neighborhood's lost children. Joshua took it all in. The history of the city, the cultures that prospered there. Occasionally a drug addict would wander by like a zombie in search of a brain to eat. He wondered why there were any poor black people in the District, a city with so much opportunity. He sipped his drink.

The rhythms ran through the crowd. Mostly Howard students and a few friends of friends. Joshua only knew Love.

Thelonius Love, but everybody simply called him Love (not to mention he hated the name Thelonius). They were from the same hometown. Love was a year older. Joshua met him at registration, holding up the line talking to an exchange student. Love looked more like a guy from D.C. and less like a guy from the Midwest: gray New Balance sneakers, gray hoodies, leather jackets, and dreads. His skin was as dark as oil and his smile beamed. He kind of reminded him of Diego, but not really.

"I'm guessing this shit is a lot different for you than that down south shit? How long you been out here now?" Love said, eyes scanning the crowd.

"Man, like three weeks. And yeah, this is way different. These houses are weird. It's a whole lot of black people. I didn't know the cost of living was so high. I might have to drop out of school and get a job. I'm so ready to be out of this place, done with school, but I can't afford it out here."

"Yeah, I know you are, son. But if you're leaving, you might want to get at some of these chicks on the Quad. You know, knock off a few of these East Coast slims first, Joe."

They both laughed.

"Naw, man. That isn't happening. You know I have a girl." Joshua adjusted his glasses. "It's not worth it. Plus, I heard the HIV rate in D.C. is outrageous."

Love nodded in agreement. "True. Me, I think I'll take my chances. It's some new chicks in here. Freshmen, I guess. Hopefully they haven't had a chance to get infected yet."

Joshua grinned, then looked around the room. There was a sea of bobs, braids, and large gold earrings. Hands went in the air and others held Styrofoam cups of spiked punch. At least one underclassman was passed out on the couch.

"I don't know about you, but I love college." Love flashed a smile. "On the real, I'm not really trying to leave, son. I have one class this semester. Did I tell you that?"

"No. Why are you only taking one class? What class is it?"

Love frowned and thought a minute. In the meantime, he

reached into an inside pocket of his vest and pulled out a half-smoked blunt and lit it. He took three or four long, deliberate drags.

"Damn, man. I don't even know. I should probably start going. What's your major?"

Joshua shook his head.

"I'm studying architecture. And if I was in your shoes, I would take advantage of this opportunity, Love. Isn't your dad a doctor or something?"

"Dentist."

"Okay, dentist. Same difference. These loans are killing me. You don't even have any loans. All you have to do is go to class. That's it! I wish that's all I had to worry about. Me and my girl, we're on our own. Her dad is sick so she's always over in P.G. She couldn't even register for class. We're struggling. I have two semesters, maybe three, but I have to pull out and find a job."

Silently, Love turned away and again began checking out the ladies in the room. He bobbed his head to the music, tapped his right foot on the hardwood floor. He took another puff and quickly began coughing, then pounding his chest.

"You want to hit this?"

"No, thanks. I don't smoke." He adjusted his glasses again. "That's all you, man. Knock yourself out."

Love smiled.

"Oh, indeed I will. Indeed, I will." He took another long drag. The sweet aroma lofted through the narrow and deep home. The distinct smell soon caught the attention of the homeowner's daughter, who was supposed to be studying with a group of friends that night, not hosting an all-night party in the Northwest D.C. house.

"Look at me," Love said. "Baggy clothes. Dreads. I look like a thug, right?"

Joshua was silent.

"Yeah, I know I do. Thing is, my grandfather was a surgeon. My grandmother owned her own business for forty years. My father is a dentist. My mother is a lawyer."

He took another pull and laughed to himself.

"I love stereotypes, Joe. I ain't no bama."

For the rest of the night, Love and Joshua talked. Love danced with girls, Joshua tried calling Kathryn. Love got buzzed, Joshua got dizzy. Love was having a ball, Joshua was ready to go. Love thought about tonight. Joshua thought about Kathryn and his future. And two days later, Kathryn's father died.

XXX

Joshua had been to funerals before. Like everybody else, he didn't like them. Two in adulthood. His grandparents' when he was a child. He didn't realize how hard Kathryn would take the passing of her father. A life-long smoker—a pack a day, like his mother—lung cancer should have been expected. *Cancer*, Joshua thought. *Fucking plague*, First his mother, now Kathryn's father. He held Kathryn's hand. She squeezed his tightly. Her wailing echoed throughout the small church. Motes floated through the air. Its wooden pews and wood floors lightly coated in a layer of dust. It irritated Joshua's nose.

A little over a week had passed since he last saw Love or the Howard campus. He thought he would probably never see either again. So there they sat. In the front row of a small, boxy church in Fort Washington, Maryland.

"Daddy!" Kathryn called out. Her voice was hoarse by this time. Her father's body lay in the casket like a gray mannequin. A sheet of spackled tears covered her face. The organ player, an old thin woman with glasses, continued with her song, the chords striking an angelic and ominous tone.

"Daddy!" she cried out.

Joshua held her hand. Patrice was having a rough go, too. She sat there quietly, but the pain showed on her face, steady streams running from her eyes. The sisters were both dressed in black. Kathryn wore a large black hat that mostly covered her eyes. Dawn looked afraid. Joshua thought this was probably her first funeral, her look indicating that she had never seen such a display of sadness and grief. She flinched every time Kathryn had an outburst. Dawn watched her like she was a foreign spectacle, a circus acrobat with a flaming sword. Joshua realized this was the first time he and Kathryn had been in a church together. He wondered what his mother would have thought, a woman who was in church every day the doors were open. He wondered if he and Kathryn should start going to church. He thought about his unpredictable work schedule and quickly dismissed the notion. Bills had to get paid.

Before this one, the most recent funeral Joshua had attended was his mother's. No one cried out there. The mood was more solemn, reserved. He remembered the leaves falling delicately on the church's windowsill. The autumn breeze tossed the orange and yellow orphans randomly. It was his senior year in high school. He would have to stay with his mother's sister, a large woman he knew only as Aunt Trell. She wasn't demanding, only asking that he go to school every day and make his bed in the morning. Aunt Trell was a good cook, like his mother. Joshua was actually very fortunate. When Lorraine died, her insurance policy at the light company guaranteed Joshua money for college. It would be his entry into State, and eventually into Kathryn's life.

"Daddy!" Kathryn was becoming weak. Joshua held her hand tighter, reassuring her that he was there. A freezing wind snuck through the church's numerous cracks. It sent a shudder through Joshua every time the cold air reached him. He held Kathryn's hand tighter. It was thinner than he remembered. The bones in her fingers were more pronounced today. The front door rattled. Dawn ducked her head under Patrice's coat. She stared at her mother's eye. Joshua noticed the little girl staring and he, too, looked at it, the extra flap of skin. The cold air snipped at his neck. He pulled his jacket tighter. The organist played her somber hymn. Joshua looked on at the body. *He was a man who had accomplished little*, Joshua thought. He didn't want that to be him. *Damn that*, he thought. The wind once again crept into the sanctuary. Joshua pulled his collar tighter. He felt Kathryn grip his hand tightly. He held hers firm.

CHAPTER 9

FEBRUARY 8, 2005
6:39 A.M.

Joshua was about ten minutes late when he made it to the group training location. There was an accident on I-395 and as usual, everyone had to slow down and stare.

"Hey, Chidu. Sorry I'm late, man. What do we have going on?" Frigid air blew in from the north. Last week's snow remained on the ground like frozen concrete. Joshua pulled up his collar to cover his neck.

"Hey, Joshua. Not much. It's cold as hell, boss. You catch that Super Bowl? Your boy McNabb choked!" Chidu let out a loud laugh.

"He's not my boy. I'm not an Eagles fan."

"Yeah, whatever. Anyway, looks like everybody's here. Yo, this one! Hot, man. Real hot. I know her."

Joshua looked up toward the parking lot. The glare of the sun and snow made it hard to see.

"Hot, huh?" Joshua laughed. "Which one? And you know her? Must be nice to be single."

"You know, it really is, boss. Sometimes when I tell chicks I'm a personal trainer, *bing*, they want to get naked in my condo. It's truly a beautiful thing, boss."

"You're a funny guy, Chidu." Joshua blew on his hands to warm them.

"Hey, guys!" Joshua yelled to the men and women, all there to shed unwanted pounds and attract the attention of others.

"Hello, gentlemen," two members of the eight-member group called out. They were all outfitted in warm nylons and fleece and caps and gloves. The winter bite nipped at their exposed parts.

"Oh shit, boss." Chidu leaned in toward Josh's ear. "That's the one I was talkin' about."

She had walked up without them noticing.

Joshua was the first to speak. He wondered why he hadn't heard the crunch of her sneakers in the snow.

"Hello, I'm Joshua Lyon. One of the personal trainers who works with Chidu."

"Hi, I'm Adelise. Pleasure to meet you."

Her hand was warm.

"Likewise. You know Chidu, right? He's a bit of a knucklehead, but we still love him."

"Yes, I know Chi. He used to work me out at this small gym in Georgetown. Wow. It is really cold out here."

"Hey, Lise. Good to see you again."

They hugged. She kissed him on both cheeks. Joshua always thought that was weird. They didn't do that sort of thing where he was from.

"That Georgetown spot was something, right. Leaky roof. I swear their yoga mats had mold on them. I see you cut your hair. Nice. And dyed it, too? I like that. Auburn, right?"

Adelise laughed.

"Thanks, Chi. I'm impressed. You know your colors. You're looking good, too. Hold on. Have you gained some weight?"

Josh chuckled under his breath. Chidu silently looked down at his midsection.

"I'm only kidding." She smiled and playfully punched him.

"Well, shall we get started?" Joshua said. "No need to be out here in the cold for too long, right? Everybody ready?" he shouted to the group, which responded in a chorus of frozen-mouthed "yeses."

"Good. You ready, Ada…Adelise? Right?"

"Yes. Like Adam Lease. Adelise."

"Cool. Got it."

"Lyon, right? Isn't that French?"

"Yes, it is. My father's side of the family was from Louisiana. Creoles. My mother called 'em geechees because they were dark. Some mess like that."

"I see. That's interesting. My father's side is from Marseille, in France. My mother is Egyptian, from Alexandria."

"You don't say? I guess that would explain it."

"Explain what?" Adelise smiled. Chilled vapor escaped her mouth.

"Nothing. Never mind." Joshua scratched his neck and pushed his glasses up.

Chidu frowned, then smiled.

"You guys ready to get started? I'm freezing my ass off out here."

Adelise looked Joshua up and down. "You know, you're very handsome. And tall. How tall are you?"

Joshua blushed. He hoped it wasn't visible. "Whoa. Where did that come from?"

"I say what's on my mind." Adelise rubbed her thighs to warm them. Joshua snuck a peek as she did. "Although I don't do glasses. You should lose those. You ever considered contacts? I think you'd be a lot more attractive without them."

"Huh? Thank you, I guess. I don't hear that often," Joshua said, scratching his neck, then awkwardly jumping in place, as if trying to warm up. "I have thought about contacts, never seriously, though. I don't like the idea of a foreign object resting on my eyeballs. Oh, and I'm about six feet two and a half. Almost six-three."

"Wow. As a model I'm usually the tallest one in the room, especially when I have heels on. And you should really think about the contacts. Trust me."

"I will. And you're a model? Chidu didn't tell me that. Yeah. Yeah, I can see that." Joshua grinned. "I always told my wife she should model. She said she was too short. And too thick. You know?"

"Oh. Your wife? I guess I didn't notice your ring." She glanced down. It was there. "She must be beautiful. You all ready to get started. It's awfully cold out here."

Joshua suddenly felt a vibration on his hip. He grabbed his cell and looked at it.

"Will you excuse me for one minute?"

"Come on, Josh. I'm dying over here," Chidu said.

"Sorry, dude. Go ahead and the get group started with a warm-up jog." Josh looked down toward the end of the pier. "Down that way. Toward the river. Then do some stretching."

Chidu nodded and led the group in a light jog down the path toward the Potomac River.

"Hey."

"Hey, honey. You made it there okay? I heard there was an accident on 395."

"Yeah, babe, I made it okay. Thanks for calling. We're about to get started."

Joshua could hear the silence on the other end. It was a long and uncomfortable silence. "Hey. Is everything okay?"

"I'm lonely, honey. I want a baby. Don't you want a little Josh running around?"

Joshua looked down the pier and could see Chidu frantically waving him down. He sighed.

"Well, babe, look. Sure, yeah. I guess. Can we talk about this when I get home?"

Kathryn paused.

"Okay. Hurry home. And drive safely. The roads are bad and I don't want to hear about you on the news."

"Yes. You told me that when I left the house. I'll drive safely. I love you. Bye."

Joshua placed his phone back on his hip. The sun had fallen behind a cloud and the air seemed colder now.

"Must be nice." Adelise was grinning. Joshua was shocked to see her standing there. "I forgot my scarf and my cap. Didn't mean to startle you."

"No, you didn't startle me. What must be nice?"

"That. Must be nice to have someone check in on you like that."

Joshua grinned. Chill in the air caused the skin on his face to tighten. "It's okay."

"You know, if I was in a relationship, I would never call my man. People say men are like dogs, but I don't believe that. I believe men are like cats. They're more finicky."

Joshua rubbed his hands together.

"Is that so?" He looked down and noticed a red gold bracelet dangling from her wrist. "That's a nice bracelet."

"Oh, this?" Adelise lifted her arm. "Thank you. It's Nefertiti.

My father gave it to me. I need to be careful running with it out here. It's a little loose. I've lost it before."

"Egyptian, right?" Joshua reached out and fingered the small gold face. "Very nice. Yeah, I wouldn't want you to lose that. Now, what were you saying about men and cats?"

"Oh, yes, it's true." Joshua could now detect a trace of an accent in her voice. For some reason, he hadn't noticed it before. "They are like cats. And just like cats, you have to give them space. If they want to come around, they will. It's really fairly simple. They leave, they come back."

"Really? I see. And are you married?" Joshua was smiling.

"No."

"And why is that?"

She smiled. "Because I lock the door, darling. Cats can't use keys."

Joshua burst into laughter. "That's pretty good."

"Guys!" Chidu yelled to them.

"Yeah!" Joshua yelled back. "Adelise? Looks like this cat is ready. Shall we begin?"

They started a slow steady jog toward Chidu and the rest of the group. Crisp air entered their lungs and burned and invigorated simultaneously. Joshua peered to his right and was surprised to see an enormous metallic hand stretching from the soil, piercing the dull gray sky.

"Wow. What is that?" His words were cold and curt.

"You've never been to Hains Point before? It's the Awakening."

They got closer and Joshua could see another hand and a foot and then a leg. The giant man's face looked pained. Agonizingly rising from the earth.

"Yeah, I've been to Hains Point before. Once. Never noticed that. That's pretty amazing."

Adelise smiled. A skullcap now concealed the top of her hair, allowing her reddish mane to flow freely around her neck, playfully caressing her scarf.

"You know, you should really get out more. But, I guess it is pretty cool. I think it's supposed to symbolize man's struggle. Almost like a rebirth. Coming to life for the first time."

They neared the group. Chidu had everyone doing jumping jacks. Joshua's and Adelise's feet rhythmically slapped the crusted snow. Their strained breaths released synchronized mists of near-frozen air.

"Yeah, that's real cool," Joshua said, turning his head back to the path and giant sculpture. "Coming to life for the first time."

CHAPTER 10

SEPTEMBER 13, 1996
6:43 P.M.

"Josh. Joshua. Wake the fuck up, dude. Let's go to the caf'." Diego's voice was deep and raspy.

Joshua tossed in his bed.

"Dude, get the fuck up! We're going to miss the caf', and I'm broke. And I know you're broke."

Joshua stirred again, then opened his eyes. "Man, Diego, why do you have to curse so much?"

"Fuck you. Let's go get some nasty-ass dinner. Get your belly full before we go out tonight and get faded. What? You tired from all those ass whoopins you took in Madden last night?"

Joshua reached over to his desk and grabbed his glasses. "Whatever. You suck. I went to class today. Three. Can you say the same?"

"I suck? Okay. You weren't saying that when I SWACed you like five times. Buffalo all in that ass. I'm the Madden champ up in here. And for your information, I didn't have class today. The one class I had got cancelled."

"Yeah. Whatever."

"Yeah, I know you really don't want any more of that Madden ass whoopin'. Man, let's go!"

Joshua looked down at his plaid shirt. He wanted to iron it

and his dingy jeans, but he didn't have time. Diego was already dressed. His goatee was trimmed and his sneakers were clean. The phone in their room began to ring.

"Dang, Diego, your fan club must be ready for the weekend, too."

"Yeah, I know. Let me answer this real quick." He picked up the phone. "What? What's up, girl? Me and my boy 'bout to hit the caf'. All right. Cool. I'll call you back later."

Diego placed the phone back on the base and smiled. His lean shoulders jutted out the sides of his T-shirt.

"See, that wasn't hard. The blaxican knows how to handle things. You ready? I'm hungry as fuck."

XXX

They rode the dorm elevator down to the lobby and walked out the building. The early evening sunlight struck them in the eyes and they both bunched their faces. Hot summer air greeted them in this Southern state.

Diego looked over at Joshua. "Man, I wish I had your height. Couple more inches, I would be dunking on fools like it's nobody's business. You don't play any sports. That's a damn shame."

"I know. I lift weights every once in a while. I do my pushups and situps."

"Yeah? Fuck that. You need to be runnin' through these broads. What you waiting for? We've been here for four *years*. You can't keep acting the way you did in high school, Joshy Josh."

Joshua smiled.

"You know that's not my style. I'm a low-key guy."

Josh and Diego suddenly saw several groups of guys talking with animated emotion. One girl ran out her dorm crying.

"What the fuck is going on?"

"Ya'll didn't hear?" one guy from the Bay Area said.

"No." Joshua was confused. "Hear what?"

"Tupac died."

Diego and Joshua stopped in their tracks. They could clearly hear the girl crying now.

"Damn. He died?"

"Yeah, man. They just reported on the news. Ya'll didn't see it?"

"Naw, man. I was sleep."

"Yeah, dude. It's messed up." The guy walked away.

Diego and Joshua started walking again. It seemed hotter now. More uncomfortable.

"Man. That was my dude. Damn. He's dead. I was sure he was going to survive this shooting; just like the last one. I can't believe he's dead. I was bumping his CD last night!"

"I know. That's sad, man. I liked his music."

"Liked it? Motherfucka, he's the best rapper ever. He's the only cat that could rap about murder and his momma in the same line. He was cold. Damn. I'm gonna miss that cat."

Joshua glanced over at Diego. They could now see more girls crying as the news spread.

"Dang," Joshua said. "This is crazy. Guess he had a lot of fans."

Diego looked at him and shook his head.

"The world is going to miss Tupac. He could rock a beat on some hood shit and them come with some positive, uplift-the-race-type shit. I gotta get a brick of MD 20/20 so I can pour out a little liquor for the homey. This is sick."

They were now right outside the cafeteria doors. An air of gloom covered the campus. Joshua and Diego waited in one of two lines to get their meal tickets. Joshua suddenly perked up.

"Oh my God!" Joshua stopped in his tracks.

"What?" Diego looked all around. "What's up?"

"Man, do you see her?"

"Who?" Joshua scanned the campus. He saw numerous coeds, football players, guys in the band, but nothing that caught his eye.

"Her! Her, man! In the red shorts. Look at those legs."

Diego caught a glimpse of red shorts in the opposite line and followed them up to her face.

"Her? Right there? The chick crying?" He pointed. "Right there? You like her?"

"Yeah, man. She's cute. Look at those legs. I've never seen her before. She must be new."

Diego frowned.

"I don't know, man. She's borderline fat. Her face is okay. She's not ugly. But she looks chunky to me. And why is she crying? Tupac didn't know her."

The girl couldn't see them talking about her. She wiped her tears. Joshua slapped Diego's arm.

"No, man. She's thick. Big boned. I think she's pretty. And I think she was checking me out."

Diego burst into laughter.

"Oh, yeah? She was checking you out? Dude, she's fucking crying. She was probably crying about you, wondering, 'who is this big black unathletic buster who is staring at me'?"

Diego's booming laugh echoed off the auditorium and cafeteria walls.

"Damn, man. You made her cry!"

"Whatever. She was checking me out. I'm serious. I saw her looking. Man, I want to meet her. You know anybody who knows her?"

Diego gathered himself. He realized Josh was serious.

"I don't think so. But if you're serious, I can find out. I think she's a Cali chick. They all wear those long braids like that. I'll find out for you."

"Cool, man. I appreciate it." Joshua went to shake his hand.

"Dude, calm down. Don't get all gay on me."

Joshua chuckled. "Whatever, Diego. Let's get something to eat."

CHAPTER 11

JUNE 29, 2008
10:21 A.M.

Joshua sat on the Metro reading a book. The train was packed with tourists. Fat Midwesterners and Southerners with beet-red skin and shorts that were too tight. Joshua looked up briefly. These were the type of people he worked with every day. Overweight. Obese. Laden with excuses. Slow metabolism. No healthy choices available to them. That's how they were raised. The greasy look of their skin made him sick. He looked back at his book, something Chidu loaned him.

I'm crazy. I think I can say that with some amount of confidence. Although many crazy, or clinically diagnosed mentally retarded, excuse me, mentally challenged, or whatever you want to call them, would probably never admit to that. They probably don't possess the capacity. But I'm crazy like a peacock. You must know, I've made a terrible mistake. A terrible, terrible mistake. I've been good thus far. Never leaving a clue. But you know how confidence is; it can lead to carelessness. I've made this little boo-boo and now what? What now?

Someone's sweaty leg rubbed against Joshua's. He looked up.

"Oh, sorry."

He went back to his book.

Well, where shall I begin? Let me start off by saying that they would never suspect me. Oh, they would probably suspect me in a pocket-

book snatching or maybe some other dumb trivial crime. But I'm a serial killer. And I'm good at it.

The train came to the next station, a transfer point for the Blue Line. A group of teens piled in, noisy and boisterous. Joshua briefly glanced at them. He went back to his book.

Would you like to know how I got started? Who wouldn't, right? I'll welcome you inside my mind for a moment, but only a brief moment. I don't have oodles of time because I have to figure out what I'm going to do about my little boo-boo.

Joshua looked out the window at the whirr of trees and townhouses. The train came to a smooth stop at the airport. Sweaty business travelers and families got on and off. Tourists melted under the blazing sun. Joshua was buried in his book when he heard someone call his name.

"Josh? Joshua Lyon?"

He thought he heard something and looked up. The face looked familiar but he couldn't place it. He looked a few years older. Well-dressed, but his skin was pock-marked. Crow's feet dug in around his eyes.

"It's me. Blaine. From Texas. We went to State together. Down south!"

His memory had been jogged.

"Oh! Blaine! From Dallas, right? I remember you. How have you been? Sit down."

Joshua moved his gym bag off the seat next to him as Blaine eased past a few riders who were standing.

"Man, I haven't seen you for years. How have you been? What happened to you, bruh?"

Joshua smiled at Blaine's accent. "I've been good. Really good. I transferred to Howard with my wife. Well, she was my girlfriend then."

"Man, that's good to hear. That's funny. You headed to work?" Blaine looked down at Joshua's clothes.

"Yea, I'm going..." He hesitated. "...to work out."

"Oh, okay. Man that's cool. I need to work out." He patted his belly. "I'm in pharmaceuticals. I do a little biotech, too. Mostly working with government contractors."

"Wow. That's real nice, man. I hear that's where the money is."

Blaine laughed. "Well, if it is, someone needs to tell the money where *I* am!"

They both laughed.

"So what you reading there? You read a lot?"

"Not really. I'm reading more now. I never used to read stuff like this. Fiction. But ever since my wife stopped working...and then the baby. I don't know. I guess sometimes I need an escape."

"Man, Josh, you're married? And got kids? That's all right. Man, you look exactly the same."

"Yeah, you look the same, too," Joshua lied. "Yep. Married. I have a son."

"Oh, man. Man, that's beautiful."

"You know, you might know my wife, Kathryn McFee. She went to State. She was from California, well, Maryland, really."

"Kathyrn McFee? Sounds familiar. Short? Like a light-brown skin? Like...real curvy?"

"She *was* curvy. But yeah, that's her."

"You married *her*?" There was such a feeling of surprise in his voice. It caught Joshua off guard. He scowled.

"Yeah, I married *her*. What does that *her* mean?"

Blaine squirmed, then smiled.

"Aw, nothing, man. Nothing. I didn't see her...I mean, you two. You know? That's all right, right there, man. That's all right. I'm really happy for you."

Blaine smiled again and turned toward the window. The train was underground now, nothing but black tunnel surrounding them. Solitary lights were halogen streaks. The hum of the train was an annoying white noise. Blaine stared blankly at the shadowy haze that was the tunnel.

Joshua chuckled. "You okay, Blaine? Man, really, what did that look mean? And the *her*?"

"Aw, nothing, man. I'm really happy for you. Kathryn McFee. That's all right," He turned toward Joshua. "You know, everyone used to call her McFine?" Blaine laughed. "She sho was fine, too."

Joshua smiled.

"Yea, I knew that was her nickname. I met her when we were seniors." Joshua paused, and thought for a second. "Damn, Blaine, is there something I should know? Your whole demeanor changed when I said I was married to Kathryn."

"Huh? Aw, naw, man. She's a good girl. She's a good one, Josh. Believe me."

But Joshua didn't believe him.

"Come on, Blaine. We used to share bologna sandwiches in the dorm freshman year. You moved off campus the next year, but still we go way back. Is there something I should know about the woman that's now my wife?"

Blaine again turned his head toward the window. The train was now fuller. People packed themselves in. It was hot and crowded. Many of the travelers were uncomfortable. Tourists with short sleeves brushed up against women in blouses, their out-of-town sweat touching the skin of the train's daily commuters.

"Man, look, Josh. I'm in town for a conference today and tomorrow. Today's seminar ends at five. What's your schedule look like this evening?"

"I'm open."

"Okay. I'm staying at the Marriott on Fourteenth. Let's meet up for drinks and catch up."

"Sounds good."

They exchanged numbers. The air in the train was becoming unbearable, especially for Joshua. It was hard for him to breathe. The musty stench smothered him.

"The next stop is mine. We'll talk tonight. Man, Josh, it was good to see you. What are the chances? Well, anyway, we'll chat more this evening."

"Okay, Blaine. Same here. Looking forward to it." He tried hard to hide his anger and frustration. The bumbling and jostling of commuters began to intensely irritate him. He couldn't focus. The thought of waiting and agonizing all day seemed unbearable. He couldn't do it. "Blaine, what stop are you getting off at?"

"Uh, National Zoo. There's a hotel up there. Conference rooms, you know? I have to change trains, at uh..." He fumbled through some papers. "Chinatown. Gallery Place."

"Look here, man. To be honest with you, I can't wait until tonight," Josh said, as the train emerged from the Virginia side of the Potomac River. Jet skis and boats sliced through the murky water below them. Trees in full bloom lined both sides of the stone fortifications to the north and south banks of the river. The rails screeched loudly as the train was dipping into a tunnel on the District side of the river.

"Huh? I couldn't hear you," Blaine said, leaning in closer.

"I said I can't wait that long, man. You're killing me. Tell me the story now. I'll ride with you."

Blaine looked around. The train made a gliding stop at L'Enfant Plaza, a foot-traffic madhouse of everyday public transit commuters and vacationing tourists. Shopping bags and briefcases struck riders while they exchanged places: some getting off, many getting on.

"Okay. Man, you know how I met Kathryn? Here's what happened. It was me and G Rock, Gerald from Brooklyn. All those Southern and West Coast chicks really dug his accent. You know she used to talk to him, right?"

"Yeah, I knew that. They were boyfriend and girlfriend, right?"

Blaine frowned. "Well, not really, man. Really, I don't know how to tell you. I mean, this is kind of uncomfortable, man."

"Blaine, come on. Just tell me. Man to man. I can handle it. I need to know, if this is something involving my wife."

Blaine looked around. The train was packed. Bodies uneasily bumped against each other.

"Okay. I don't think they were together like that. I mean, I think they just fooled around. Anyway, me and G Rock, we was cool. I stopped by his place every now and then. You know, he stayed off campus, so that was the place to be."

Joshua shifted in his seat. He scratched his neck.

"So, one night I stopped by and Kathryn was there. I think they had been drinking. She wasn't much of a drinker. Had two drinks, I think. She was drunk when I got there. Well, anyway, I'm sorry, Josh, but to make a long story short, all three of us kind of did our thing."

Joshua inhaled deeply. He drove his nails into his neck, causing it to lightly bleed. "Damn, man. What are you saying? Ya'll took turns fucking my girl? I don't believe it, man. I can't believe it!"

The rumbling buzz of the train resounded through the cars. The human mass now seemed to close in on Joshua, suffocating him. He tried to catch his breath.

"Naw, man. We didn't take turns. It was more like..." Blaine paused. He pulled his suit jacket tighter. "It was more like, at the same time. You know? I'm sorry, man. For some reason, I don't know. I thought you knew."

Joshua sat there empty. "I can't believe it. You thought I knew? How would I know?"

"I mean, G Rock wasn't the most discreet dude I knew. He talked a lot. Plus, State was a small school. We figured you knew. Shit, other people knew. You know, word got out about her... about her skills."

Joshua gave Blaine a cold look. He gritted his teeth. "What? Look, man, I just can't believe it. I can't."

Blaine looked up at the Metro map. His stop was coming up. He glanced back at Josh.

"Didn't Kathryn have a tattoo? An angel, right? On the back of her shoulder?"

Joshua leaned back in his seat. His book fell to the floor.

"Yeah, I remember she did. I can still see my hand pressing down on that angel. I'm sorry, Josh. I'm sorry, man."

The train slowed at Blaine's stop and he got ready to get off.

"Sorry, man. Take care, Joshua. Don't hold anything against Kathryn. She was young. We all were. We had been drinking. Just..." He stopped. "Just don't hold it against her, man. You guys have a life together. And a child. Take care, Josh. Don't hold it against her."

He stepped off the train and in a flash, Josh watched as Blaine and the people on the platform got smaller and smaller and then disappeared in the darkness of the tunnel. He looked around. Everything was strange now. He was an outsider in a strange land. What was he doing on a subway? In the Mid-Atlantic? Married. Living there. Who were these people surrounding him? Foul smelling and clueless. Business people and government employees. Capitol Hill staffers. Aligned with a political philosophy they would defend with their lives. *They were lost*, he thought. He, too, would defend his philosophy; his wife and his son. His life. Now, he was like them. He was lost, too. He tried to orient himself. He reached for his book. He dusted it off. He tried to read, not sure where he had left off.

One day, something in me just clicked. Well, it's more complicated than that. We'll discuss that later. I assure you, all will be revealed in due time. Yes. I'm crazy.

Joshua could feel tears welling in his eyes. He fought them back with great intensity. These strangers, in this strange land, could not see him cry. He would not allow it. He held back the tears. He tried to read again.

They are looking into a double murder on the west side. Two Mexican girls. Teenagers, to be exact. They found them with their heads severed. Never found the heads, though. Nor the murder weapon. Maybe they should just ask me. The heads are in the Missouri River. Right where I put them. Probably being eaten on by fish.

Joshua began to feel nauseous. He scratched his neck. It pained him. He tried to read more.

But I've made a mistake. I left one little girl alive. I know she can identify me. I know. I'll surely go to jail. And you know what they do to child killers in jail? I can't have that. No. I know. And the answer is yes. I want to stop killing. Oh! But do not be fooled, my friend. I do have one more killing in me. There's just one left. One little-bittie delicate flower. I know. I would like to end it.

Yes. Yes, I would. I'm going to pluck the petals of her adorable life. I'm going to end this. Tonight.

Joshua closed the book and stared out the window at the bleary image that was the world moving fast.

CHAPTER 12

JULY 3, 2008
1:13 P.M.

It flapped there in the wind. Right in front of her. On the passenger side of Joshua's Toyota. A little white slip of paper. Lodged between the dashboard and the windshield. A crack in the window allowed the breeze to come in and harass it. So it flapped there, annoying Kathryn. What was it? She tried to ignore it.

"Anyway, I just like it. It's entertaining. And you? The movie you always watch?"

Joshua laughed. "What can I say? It's a great movie. Remember that time we went to see *Saw* at the movies? I thought you were going to pee on yourself!"

"I was!" Kathryn burst into laughter. "I told you I didn't like scary movies. The last one I saw was *The Exorcist*. That was it for me. No way."

"Yeah, somebody at work told me those stairs the priest fell down are in Georgetown. You want to go?"

Kathryn gave Joshua a look that said it all.

"Oh, okay," he said with a chuckle. He gently rubbed a finger on the nape of her neck. She smiled.

The little white slip of paper flapped loudly now. What the hell was it? All she knew was, it was annoying. The constant fluttering was bothering her. Slapping. She leaned forward and grabbed it.

"What's that?" Joshua looked over and saw his wife holding a small scrap of paper. She wasn't looking at it. She was examining it. "Honey, is that…?"

He looked back toward the Beltway. The racetrack on both sides whizzed in controlled chaos.

"You went to the Omni? Last week?"

"Omni," the baby repeated.

Joshua grinned. He checked the rearview mirror. "The Omni? No. What are you talking about? What's the piece of paper?"

Kathryn's chest rose as she took in a long, deep breath. She exhaled it, slowly. She pursed her lips. She looked up. Joshua looked over at her, then back at the road. He scratched his neck.

"Don't sit there and scratch your goddamn neck, Joshua. Why are you scratching? Are you nervous? Are you? Joshua, it's a fucking receipt from the Omni Shoreham Hotel's parking garage. Why were you parked at the Omni?"

"The Omni, daddy." Little Josh smiled. The strap of his overalls hung off his chubby shoulder.

Joshua looked up at the exit sign on the highway.

"Honey, which exit do I take for Tysons? I always forget."

"I don't give a fuck about the goddamn exit!" Kathryn yelled. Her light-brown hair fluttered about her head. "What the fuck were you doing at the Omni, Josh?"

"Omni, Daddy!" Little Josh laughed loudly.

"Look! Me and Chidu went to a bar over there. There was nowhere to park so I parked at the Omni. You know how bad parking is in D.C.!"

"Parking?! Josh, the date is on here. This is the same night you didn't get home until six in the morning, you asshole. I hate you!"

She started swinging her fists at him. Cars on both sides

zoomed by like rogue darts. Joshua struggled to avoid her blows and still keep the car in its lane.

"Stop it, Kathryn! Stop it! I will crash this car right now! Is that what you want? Is that what you want? You want me to crash?"

"No, Mommy. Don't hurt Daddy." The little boy frowned. "No hurt."

Kathryn seethed. "How dare you, goddamn it? How fucking dare you!"

She swung furiously at him, striking glancing blows to his shoulders and face. The Beltway was its usual spectacle of in-and-out dashes and speeding trucks, but none of that mattered to Kathryn. The baby started crying.

"No, Mommy. No!"

"Stop it, damn it! I'm gonna crash the car." Joshua reached out with his right hand to grab her arms, but he could only manage to get ahold of one. Their small four-dour rocked back and forth on the highway as the traffic around them whirred at seventy-five miles per hour. Little Josh's crying became louder and more intense.

"Let go of me! Is that what those bitches like? For you to grab them? Squeeze 'em to death? Let my fucking arm go!"

Joshua finally released her arm, again focusing his attention on the road.

"So, you had some bitch in here? In this raggedy, old-ass Toyota? What? You paid for the parking and she paid for the room? I know your broke ass couldn't afford a room at the Omni."

Kathryn suddenly began to search throughout the passenger side. She checked everything. The glove compartment. The center console. Under the mat. The baby's crying began to ease.

"Kathryn, what are you doing?" Joshua asked, now calm. "What are you looking for? You're not going to find anything, okay? No one was in here."

She silently kept moving things and searching. She opened a few CD cases. She checked the pocket in the door. She lifted up from the seat and checked the space between the chair and the driver's side. Then she saw it.

She stretched her fingers for it. The middle finger felt for it, then the index caressed it. She had it. She pulled it up. The day of light struck it: a red gold bracelet. The face of Nefertiti stared back at Joshua.

"Who the fuck does this belong to, Joshua?"

He silently exited the highway.

"Take me home, Joshua. I'm not going to the fucking mall! Take me home right fucking now!"

Joshua took the next turn and headed back to their apartment without saying another word.

CHAPTER 13

JULY 26, 2008
9:12 P.M.

"Kathryn! I'm so glad you could make it. I'm turning thirty, girl!" Charlene gave her a big hug. Her black curly hair hung down to her shoulders. Her breath smelled of wine. "Come in! Get out of that rain!"

"I know, girl. It's coming down in buckets! Where can I put my umbrella?"

"Just put it over there in the foyer. Where's Josh and Roxanne? I thought they were coming with you?"

"I know. She couldn't make it. Girl, I could barely make it. I'm tired and I had to ask my sister to watch little Josh."

"Oh, should have brought the little cutie. How is Patrice?"

"Please. That little cutie likes his daddy because I'm the disciplinarian. Patrice is good."

"That's funny. So Joshua couldn't watch him?" Charlene closed the door and led Kathryn into the dining room where several people were gathered having drinks and talking.

"Char, don't get me started on Josh. You know I just moved back in?" Kathryn threw her purse on the sofa. "He's at work, supposedly. But never mind him, can a girl get a drink up in here?"

"Of course, girl. And no, I didn't know you just moved back in. What happened?"

"Long story. I found some, uh, paraphernalia in the car. Me

and the baby were at Roxanne's place for a few days, then over to my sister's for a week. She started getting all motherly on me, so I decided to move back. Plus, I didn't have any transportation." Kathryn thought about the conversation she'd had with Joshua the previous day.

xxx

"Kathryn, this is stupid. Come home."

"Stupid? You think this is stupid? You spending the night with another woman is stupid. What were you thinking?"

Joshua was silent. He calmly scratched his neck. "Look, we didn't do anything. I swear. We only talked."

Kathryn took a bite out of her cheesesteak sandwich, then took a sip of Arnold Palmer. She wiped an onion from her lip.

"Talked?" She laughed. "You must think I'm an idiot, Josh. Really. You must think I'm stupid."

"I'm serious, Kathryn. Come home. I miss you and the baby. How is he? Is he getting big?"

She smirked. "It's been two weeks, Josh. Two weeks. He's not ready to drive yet, okay?"

"Well, how am I supposed to know? I've been trying to reach you. You don't answer your cell phone. I call the house and Roxanne says you're not there. She could be a little nicer, too. I'm always polite when she calls here. She can't be cordial?"

"Cordial? You cheated on me, Joshua! Why should she be cordial to you? We're not even there now anyway. We're at Patrice's. But do you even deserve cordialness? I don't even know if that's a word!"

Joshua stood up from the dining room table and looked out

the window. A bird pruned itself in a bush. Ants gathered crumbs in their jaws and escaped to their den. He stared at them. He thought about their purpose.

"Look. I'm sorry, Kathryn. You're my best friend. I love you very much and I miss you. Please come home. Little Joshua needs to be with his father. And you need to be with your husband. I don't want you to think..." He stopped.

"You don't want me to think what?"

"I don't want you to think something is going on. It's not. Please trust me. I mean, I've heard things about yo..." He stopped again.

Kathryn finished off her sandwich and began eating a large slice of chocolate cake.

"You heard things about what?"

Joshua watched the ants disappear into a tiny hole. "Nothing. Come home, honey. Please. Let's start over. Me and you."

There was a long silence on the phone. Joshua could hear Kathryn's fork scraping the plate. She licked the remaining chocolate icing off the fork. She laid it down and stared at the white saucer.

"I don't know, Josh." She stared at the blank plate. "Why did you do it?"

"I don't know."

"You don't know?"

"No. I don't. She was there. She complimented me. She was beautiful and complimented me." He paused. "You don't compliment me."

Kathryn pulled the phone away from her ear and looked at it. "I don't compliment you?"

"No. You don't. Look, that's not important. Nothing happened and I want you home. I really miss you and the baby. You don't miss me? Our inside jokes? Ms. Parker?"

Kathryn shook her head. "I don't know."

"Come home, honey. Please. Like I said, let's start over. Me and you." Joshua turned to sit down again. "Can you forgive me? I miss my friend."

"I don't know, Joshua."

"Kathryn, please."

"I don't know. I'll have to think about it."

XXX

Kathryn looked up at Charlene with a despondent face.

"Oh, God. Damn, Kathryn. I'm sorry to hear that. You seem to be holding up okay. Look at you, all thin. You lost all that baby weight, and then some. You on the Atkins diet?"

"No." Kathryn finally smiled. "I simply watch what I eat."

"I see. Well, you can stop watching it so much. You've watched enough. You get any smaller and your ass is going to disappear."

They both laughed.

"Kathryn, do me a favor? Take your shoes off and leave them by the door? I don't want you tracking rainwater and dog shit all over my hardwood floors. Thank you."

The block of rowhouses where Charlene lived in Southeast D.C. had been recently renovated. New cabinets. Granite countertops. Recessed lighting. The neighborhood was still in need of many basics, like a grocery store. Charlene returned with Kathryn's drink.

"Thanks. I like your place. It's roomy."

"Thank you. You want the tour?"

Kathryn took a sip of wine. The sweet berries pleased her. She could hear a television in the background.

"Okay."

They left the living room and headed toward the dining room, where a small group of Charlene's friends—and some she didn't know—had gathered to discuss politics and the war.

"Hey everyone, this is my friend Kathryn. We used to work at the Pentagon together."

"Hello," a man wearing a white linen blazer said.

"Hi," said a woman with a low haircut, nearly shaved.

The others smiled or nodded.

"So this is the dining room. As you can see, I don't have shit in here. Only this credenza. A few wineglasses and serving platters in there."

Charlene led Kathryn through the French doors that opened up to the kitchen. In the middle of the room was a granite-topped island with a deep-basin sink. Kathryn took a bigger sip of wine.

"You want something to eat?" Charlene asked, bunching her brow. "You look hungry, not to mention you're drinking alcohol."

Kathryn smiled. "No, I'm okay. It's just wine."

A crackle of thunder exploded outside.

"Okay. If you say so. Well, this is the kitchen. I still don't do a lot of cooking."

Charlene walked over near the door that led to the backyard and flipped the porch light.

"This is the backyard. I threw some wings on the grill last week."

"Oh, you did? I bet that was nice."

"It was nice. I should have invited you. I don't know why I didn't."

Kathryn tipped her glass up and drank the rest of her wine. She patted her lips together, savored the last drop of the fermented fruit.

"That wine was really good."

"Thanks, girl. You want another glass?"

"Yeah, okay. I'm not much of a drinker but I haven't been out in so long. Seems like I stay cooped up in that small apartment all day with the baby. Feeding him. Making sure he doesn't get into anything. Taking him to the park. It's hard work. You'll see when you have kids. You still single? It seems like we haven't spoken in forever. How long has it been?"

"At least a few months," Charlene said as she refreshed Kathryn's drink.

"At least. I'm really glad you called. Your place is beautiful. Hopefully, we can get a place like this one day. I guess I might need to get a job before we can do that. Is it expensive over here?"

"Girl, it's not bad. The prices are going up, though. It's still the most affordable area in D.C., and in Southeast."

Charlene took a seat at one of the barstools near the island. She grabbed a stuffed jalapeño and took a bite.

"Well, if you're not eating, at least have some dessert? I have some sorbet in the freezer."

"No, I'm okay. That's too cold for me, anyway."

Charlene chuckled. "Too cold?"

"Yeah, my teeth have gotten sensitive in my old age."

Charlene's face showed a brief look of concern, but she didn't want to linger on the topic. "So, you're still not working?"

Kathryn took the glass away from her lips. Half of the wine was already gone. "No, girl. I just can't. After nine-eleven, I don't know. I can't bring myself to do it. I was getting counseling for a while. Then I quit, my benefits ran out, and Josh's plan at the gym doesn't cover mental health. Not unless it's court ordered. Our health system sucks."

She finished the rest of her wine. "Wow. I didn't know that."

"Yep. They'll handle bullshit. Pay for that. But not mental health. Like it's a joke. I think Joshua thinks I'm faking it. Making it up, something. Like I don't want to work. Does he think I like being broke? You see this dress?"

Charlene looked at her outfit. She really hadn't paid attention to it at first. "Yes. It's nice."

"Consignment shop. They have a little place in Del Ray in Virginia. The shoes, too. Does he think I like being broke? Riding around in his beat-up car with the dirty car seat in the back?"

Rain came down and showered the backyard darkness. Thunder rolled in the distance.

"I mean, I would work. I would work. But I just can't. I can't bring myself to sit at a desk. I can still hear that awful explosion. I thought I was going to die in there. So many people died that day. My God. I will never forget that day. Never forget it."

"I know. It was crazy. It was hard on me, too. But you know, sometimes you just have to get back in there. Get on with life. Life does go on."

Kathryn stared at her glass, the purple streaks, nearly invisible, that clung to the sides.

"You want another glass?" Charlene asked.

"No. No, I'm okay for now." Kathryn set the glass down.

Charlene smiled. "You guys should think about moving over here. Like I said, it's still really affordable. I don't know how much Josh makes, but you all should be okay."

"Not enough, girl. He doesn't make enough. Plus, we have the baby. Is it safe over here? You know, for kids?"

"I haven't had any problems. You have weirdos that walk around, but a lot of the riffraff have moved out. 'Cause you know you have people like Madison moving in." Charlene pointed at the cheery redhead in the living room.

"That's my next-door neighbor. She's really nice. She's from California, too. Up north by San Francisco, I think. Did I tell you Madison and I are trying to get a petition signed to get a Starbucks around here?"

Kathryn giggled.

"No. You didn't tell me that." She laughed again. "I could see you doing that, though. Girl, it is so good to see you."

They hugged.

"I know. It's really good to see you, too. You got me over here thinking about September eleventh. I'm ready to drink now! This is my birthday party!"

Charlene got up and walked to the dining room where everyone was still chatting and sipping their drinks. Kathryn slowly stood and followed behind her.

"Who wants to take a shot with me?" Charlene asked everyone in the room.

"I'll take one with you," said the man in the white blazer.

"Cool! I knew I could count on you, Tommy. Anybody else?"

Everyone else shook their head.

"I'll take one," Kathryn said. "Why not? It's your birthday, right?"

Charlene stared at her for a second. "Are you sure? I think those two glasses of wine have already gotten you nice."

"No. No, I'm good. I'll take one." Kathryn brushed her sandy hair back behind her ear. "What are we drinking?"

"Tequila. Patron," Charlene said. "Have you had it before?"

"No. But I think I heard of it." Kathryn smiled brightly. "Let's do it!"

Charlene sliced three lime wedges and lined up the shot glasses. Kathryn grabbed the salt from the kitchen. With the drinks poured, Tommy and the girls downed the first round. Charlene frowned. So did Kathryn, but she thought it was smooth.

"That wasn't bad," Kathryn said, staring at the small shot glass. "Okay. Let's do one more, then I'm done."

Charlene snickered. Kathryn could see the television on the living room. She caught a glimpse of Devin Gentle.

"Oh! That's my show!" She quickly found a seat in front of the television.

"You watch that?" Charlene sounded amazed.

"Yeah, girl. I love this show. This is my little escape from reality. I've missed the last couple of weeks, but this looks like a rerun. Good." She turned up the volume.

"Having chugged the remainder of my cocktail, I place an order for another dirty martini and wait patiently while the soft classical music in the background filters into my ears. The pleasurable tone is interrupted by the last thing I wanted to hear: 'So you're a writer and a private investigator?' the gentleman belts with a commanding CEO type of voice."

"Girl, this is the one I left off on," Kathryn said, sounding thrilled.

"That's good." Charlene walked over and began mingling with her other guests.

"I respond in the affirmative. Wafts of citrus and ginger fill my noise. I'm nearly tempted to ask him what he's wearing, but the ultra-straight mid-westerner in me forbids it. It's Creed, I suspect.

"'I once thought about writing a book,' he states, gulping huge

amounts of vodka on the rocks. Droplets trickle down his wide chin as he wipes them away with his manicured right hand. His black Armani tux probably used to fit perfectly. He begins an attempt to regale me with his stories of adventures on the high seas, his run-in with the law in Malaysia, and his harrowing discussions with a high-ranking Chinese government official. But soon enough, all I can make out is 'blah, blah, blah, seas. Blah, blah, blah, blah, official.'

"Wow, that's exciting," I deadpan. Then I see her. Actually, I see her seeing me. The same gray mistress that ambushed me is now chatting her up. Her wavy black hair looks similar to the rolling waves in the dark Hudson River forty floors below. As I try not to stare at her, a warm mink stole passes by and bumps the drink I just received from the barkeep.

"My libation is safe, but I am simultaneously pleased and annoyed by the sheer softness of the fur jostling. I want to look at the woman who bumped me, but I dare not lose eye contact with the lovely dame across the way. Her face is smooth. Her lips looking as if they taste like cherry pie. I'd wager her scent is one of jasmine or some exotic Persian oil.

"'Blah, blah, blah, blah, blah, right? Am I right?' The man chuckles and he slaps my right shoulder with a firm teammate-like swipe.

"'I see what you're saying,' I respond, hoping my generic statement will satisfy whatever he was asking.

Her almond-shaped eyes are perfectly colored, resembling bright jade with flecks of amber. Egyptian? Iranian? Her shawl is made of the finest red silk, trimmed in tiny golden leaflets that hang ever so sublimely on her toned beige shoulders. I prepare to heroically rescue her from the She-Cougar and introduce myself, imagining my skills result in us rolling around in a giant canopy bed with burgundy satin sheets and rose petals strewn about. Several other thoughts race through my head. For instance, I wonder if she's a fan of Russia's great Leo?"

XXX

A vibration suddenly emitted from Kathryn's purse on the sofa. She didn't hear it. But the woman with the short hair did.

"Excuse me. Excuse me. I think your phone is ringing."

Kathryn didn't hear her. The short woman walked over and grabbed Kathryn's purse and tried to hand it to her. "Hey, excuse me. I think your phone was ringing."

Kathryn's face turned vicious. "What the fuck are you doing with my purse? I don't know you like that! Charlene, you better get this bitch. You better tell her she don't know me. I'm from Inglewood. I don't play that shit." Kathryn snatched her purse and stumbled on the shiny wood floor, nearly losing her balance.

"I'm sorry, Asa. She's drunk." Charlene tried to smooth it over. "She didn't mean that."

Asa turned away from them without speaking and walked toward the dining room and her date.

"Kathryn, that's my girl. Chill. Okay? Don't get all Cali on us."

"Girl, you know I will. I'm trying to be a lady. Shit. I'm a married woman now. But your girl doesn't know me like that. Touching my purse. What if I have a vibrator or something in here? I will still put my hands on a bitch. Don't trip."

Charlene grinned. Kathryn's phone started to vibrate again. This time she unzipped her purse and answered it.

"Hello?"

"Kat. Kat? What are you doing?"

"Shit. Talking to my girl, Charlene. What's going on?"

"You sound drunk. What time are you coming to get Josh? I'm only asking because I need to run to the store, and you know my brakes are bad. Can you take us when you come to get him?"

Kathryn checked her watch.

"Okay. I'm going to leave now. I should be there in about twenty minutes."

"Okay, thanks. And drive carefully. D.C. cops don't mess around. And neither does P.G."

She snapped the phone shut.

"Girl, I have to get the baby and run my sister to the store. Right after I take this last drink." Kathryn quickly threw the liquor down her throat. She didn't feel the burn this time.

"Are you sure you can drive? Can Patrice go ahead and watch Joshua overnight? You can stay here."

"No. No. It's okay. She has to work tomorrow, anyway. I'm fine, girl. I'm fine. I'll see you next time." Kathryn grabbed her umbrella and headed for the door. "Thanks for having me. Sorry I cursed your friend out."

XXX

The roadway was a wet, black mystery. A glossy, shiny creature soaked in falling rain. The wiper blades on the Toyota were run down. Kathryn put them on the highest setting. And even then she still strained to see through the downpour. The liquor saturated her frail system. It took every ounce of her concentration to stay on the road. Every few minutes, she swerved out of her lane, momentarily losing her focus. Many drivers had avoided the streets that night due to the relentless rain. The empty highway was probably the only way she was able to make it to Patrice's house in Temple Hills, Maryland. She pulled into the driveway and blew the horn.

XXX

"Hey."

"Hey. Dawn, put your seatbelt on," Patrice said. "It's raining cats and dogs." She quickly strapped the sleeping baby in his car seat, then got in. A smudge of creamy cheese stained his cheek. Patrice tossed her umbrella to the floor. "How was the party?"

"Nice. It was nice. Her place is nice."

Patrice stared at her little sister. The extra flap of skin over her eye seemed more pronounced. Kathryn didn't want to look at it. The driving rain sounded like pennies dancing on the roof.

"Are you drunk? You're slurring your words. Kathryn, maybe you shouldn't be driving."

"No. No, I'm good. Just had a glass of wine. Where we going?"

"One glass? I guess. Take us to McDonald's. I was going to cook something but to hell with that. It's too late and I'm too tired."

"McDonald's? Oh, that sounds good," Kathryn said as she pulled onto the road. The pavement was black and slick. "I could eat a double cheeseburger, some fries, a milkshake, maybe a couple apple pies, too."

Patrice looked at her.

"How have you been, Dawn?" Kathryn said, looking at the girl in the rearview.

"Fine."

"How's your summer going?"

"Good."

"That's good." Kathryn squinted her eyes under the blaze of streetlights. The occasional car in the opposite lane blinded her. She struggled to stay focused.

"Kathryn, you want me to drive? You look like you're on one." Patrice looked over at her sister. She always thought Kathryn looked like their mother. Short. Light skinned. It annoyed her. For her Kathryn was a constant reminder that their mother ran off to be with another man. "Kathryn, can you even see?"

"I'm fine, Patrice. You just sit there and ride." Kathryn cracked the window. She needed to feel the wet breeze.

"How's Joshua doing?"

"Girl, who knows? He's been acting so damn strange lately. I can't take it. I don't know. I think he's still upset that I'm not working. Saying that we could have more, if I got a job. I don't know. He really thinks post-traumatic stress disorder is a dang joke. It's not. I can't even function in a work setting anymore. I don't know. I guess we need to have a sitdown. Maybe there's something I can do. I do want more out of life. You know?"

Patrice nodded.

"I don't know. We need to talk, I guess. He is my friend. And I do love him. We just need to talk. We'll see. I want this thing to work."

Kathryn's stomach felt a little queasy. She could taste old wine in the back of her mouth. She rolled the window down some more. She was feeling tired now. Worn down by the alcohol. Sheets of rain continued to pound them. She fought to see through the millions of drops. The dark night was uninviting.

"So, Dawn, what grade will you be in when school—"

"Kathryn, look out!"

***

Maybe it was the rain, or the dark of night, or the alcohol that she had consumed (or a combination of the three), but whatever the reason, Kathryn didn't see the stop sign. Was it obscured? Blocked by a looming bush? She sped through the intersection. The truck that smashed into the passenger side didn't see her coming. Patrice saw it. But it was too late. It took Joshua and Chidu more than half an hour to get to the hospital after they got the call. Roxanne managed to get there before them. They saw her in the emergency department waiting room. She was disheveled.

"How are they?" Joshua asked.

He could tell she had been crying.

"It's not good, Joshua. It's not good."

Joshua went to the front desk.

"I'm Joshua Lyon. You brought my wife and son here. Kathryn Lyon and Joshua Lyon. And my sister-in-law and niece. Patrice McFee and Dawn McFee."

***

"Hello, Miss. I'm Chidu. Heard a lot about you. You okay?" Chidu rubbed her shoulder.

"I'm fine. Just a little shaken up. That's my girl and her family in there. Might as well be my family in there, for real."

"No doubt. I understand. They'll be okay. They'll be fine. Let's have a seat."

A young nurse slowly escorted Joshua to E.D. bay fourteen. He wondered what she could possibly know about emergency medicine. He was suddenly nervous for Kathryn and his son. The emergency department was eerily quiet. The white floors and walls seemed to glow under the bright onslaught of large lights.

"Your wife is here. You son is in the next bay. Right now he's in fair condition. But we're monitoring him in the event that we need to transfer him to Children's. The doctor will be in shortly to speak with you."

"Thank you."

He walked in and Kathryn was attached to several monitors. She had several light scratches on her face, where flying glass had nipped her. There was an IV in her arm. Her eyes were closed. He could smell that familiar hospital scent like salty blood. Kathryn's eyes were closed. She looked peaceful. That angered Joshua. He turned to go to the next room to see Josh junior. His steps were loud.

"Joshua."

He stopped.

"Hey, honey. I got here as soon as I could. How are you feeling?"

"Terrible. How's Patrice and the baby?"

"I don't know yet. The baby's next door. It sounded like he's going to be okay."

Joshua stood next to Kathryn, looking down on her. He felt resentment. "Am I the only one trying, Kathryn? Why are we in a hospital emergency department?"

Kathryn looked confused. She shook her head. She appeared speechless at first, then hurt. "Why are you asking me this? *Now*? You don't know what it's like, Joshua. Where's your compassion for *me*? I'm still hurting from that day. It doesn't go away. I lived through the most terrifying thing on September eleventh. It's now the second most terrifying thing. You think I meant to put my son in harm's way?"

Joshua craned his neck.

"You can't keep going on like this. You almost killed our son!" Joshua raised his voice. "I don't even know how Dawn and Patrice are doing! Nine eleven was seven years ago! Get over it!"

Kathryn turned away from him and faced the monitor that was connected to her heart rate. Two lines, one red and one green, jutted in mountainous peaks and valleys. She sighed.

"You treat me like I'm faking it. Like I'm some big hypochondriac. Like I should be just fine."

"Other people are fine, Kathryn. A lot of other people have gone on—"

"I'm not other people! I didn't have a caring, loving family growing up. No one cared for me. No one cooked for me. No one looked out for me. No one cared about me! Now, my husband, the man I love, is treating me like a goddamn pariah. You hate me!"

Joshua scratched his neck. "I don't hate you, Kathryn. I love you. I love you so much that I want the best for you. I want you to get well. I want us to have a home one day. A big beautiful one. I want more children with you. I really do. But we have to be able to move on. You have to get past that day. I'll help you. Okay? We can get past that day. You have to also start taking care of yourself. You have to eat better. You're looking too thin, honey. It doesn't look healthy. I am here for you. Trust me. I'm here for you."

He reached out and grabbed her hand. It was cold and damp. He could see she was crying.

"Mr. Lyon?"

Joshua looked up. The doctor was a brown-skinned man with glasses. He was clean shaven. Joshua thought he was probably Indian.

"Yes?"

"I'm Doctor Chetty. Can you please come out into the hall with me?"

"I'll be back, honey."

"Okay," Kathryn said, wiping her eyes.

XXX

The doctor led Joshua back down the hall to a small room with a table and several chairs in it. He closed the door behind them.

"It looks like your wife will be fine. Your son sustained some head trauma. It appears to be only minor, though. We're going to keep both of them here for observation overnight."

Joshua nodded. He rubbed his hands together.

"Your niece will be fine, too. I actually think she can go home tonight. Not even a scratch on her."

"Okay. That's good to know."

"Yes, it is. I guess it's bittersweet, though."

Joshua was unsure of the doctor's words.

"'Bittersweet'?"

The doctor frowned. "You haven't heard? Your sister-in-law didn't make it. She's gone."

"Gone?"

"She was D.O.A. She died at the scene. I'm afraid she took the brunt of the impact. Does..." He looked down at the chart in his hands. "Does Dawn have a relationship with her father? Your wife's friend Roxanne was very helpful, but she didn't have an answer to that."

Joshua sat there in disbelief.

"Mr. Lyon?"

"No. She doesn't. They don't speak. Does my wife know that her sister is gone?"

"No. That sort of news is not conducive for the healing process. We will leave it up to you how to best tell her."

Joshua sighed. There was suddenly a knock on the door. It opened.

"Doctor Chetty, decel in fifteen."

"Excuse me," he said to Joshua.

Joshua sat there for a moment. *Damn*, he thought. *Patrice*. He then heard the shuffling of feet, the soft rubber-soled shoes they all wore made a distinctive sound on the smooth linoleum flooring. *Fifteen*, he thought. *Fifteen. Josh!*

He stood and bolted from the small room as fast as he could. He could see a flurry of activity down the long hall in the room next to Kathryn's. He was breathing heavy. His shoes slapped the ground.

"Please, sir, wait out here," one older nurse barked. Her breath was foul.

"That's my son! What's happening?"

"His pulse has dropped. Please, you have to wait out here!"

"But that's my son! That's my little man."

"Please, sir."

"But that's my son." Joshua's eyes began to pour tears. "That's my little boy."

CHAPTER 14

OCTOBER 19, 1996
8:33 P.M.

Her room smelled intoxicating, a pungent mix of flowers and incense. She had cleaned up before he arrived, putting away her sweatpants and her tennis shoes. He sat there, unsure of what to do next. He was nervous.

"Did you like the movie?" Kathryn asked. She smiled at Joshua. Her hair was pulled up in a neat bun.

"Yeah. It was funny. That was my first time seeing *Friday*." Joshua grinned. "Smokey! Smokey!"

Kathryn laughed.

"Good thing you have a car. We wouldn't have been able to get to Wal-Mart to rent it."

"Yeah." Joshua grinned. "The good ole Toyota comes in handy."

"Yes, it does. Hi, Ms. Parker," Kathryn said in a flattering voice, imitating the movie. Joshua laughed. "You're silly, Joshua. I like you. You're a really nice guy. Must be a Midwestern thing."

"You do?" Joshua scratched his neck. "I mean, that's cool. I like you, too. I really like your smile. But, yeah, I don't know. My mother always taught me to be a gentleman. And I guess, lucky for me, Diego knew somebody who knew your roommate. But Diego knows a lot of people, so that didn't surprise me."

He nudged his glasses up and looked around the room. She

had a poster of the Los Angeles skyline above her bed. Across from that hung a collage of photos of her friends from high school—Roxanne and Patrice—and photos of new friends from State. Her small twin bed squeaked every time Joshua shifted his weight. They had been hanging out for more than two weeks now. This was their first time alone together. Joshua's anxiety was palpable.

"So how's the liberal arts thing going?"

"Pretty good. I really have no idea what I'm going to focus on. I don't know. I guess I just want a degree. Then maybe my father can get off my back."

"Oh really?"

"Yeah. He's pretty much an asshole. I mean, he sends me a little money here and there for laundry and to eat, but other than that, we really don't speak."

"Oh," Joshua said. He picked at his fingernails.

"And you? Engineering, right? How's that going?"

"Architecture. It's going pretty good. I want to build houses for a living, so that's the field to be in."

"Oh. Wow! I didn't know that. That sounds cool. House builder and shit." Kathryn giggled. "So are you close to your family?"

"Well, my mother passed away when I was in high school. She had cancer. I went to stay with my aunt, but I was pretty much old enough then to take care of myself. When I go home, I stay with my aunt, but I don't really have anyone else there."

"I'm sorry to hear about your mom. My mother left me and my sister when we were young, just ran off. My dad raised us. He always had different women in and out of the house. He had one woman teach me and my sister how to put on our first bras, and another one showed us how to use tampons."

"Really?" Joshua looked uncomfortable.

"Yep. But, whatever. You roll with it, right?" She smiled at him. "You're easy to talk to."

"I am?" Joshua smiled.

"Yeah. You really are. You know visitation ends soon?" She leaned closer to him. "We'll have to go downstairs in a few minutes."

"I know."

She leaned over and kissed him. He flinched.

"Are you okay?"

"Yeah. Yeah, I'm okay." He chuckled. "I just didn't expect that."

"Did you like it?"

"Yes."

He moved closer and kissed her lips. Then her cheek. Then her neck. A small curl hung down the back of her neck. Joshua caressed it. She moaned. She placed her arms around him and pulled him closer. Their tongues danced. She reached down for his belt. His belly quaked. She unzipped his jeans and caressed him. He was aroused. He reached under her skirt and pulled her white panties down. She lifted her back off the bed to help them slide off smoothly. He looked her in the eyes. He gently pushed her head back onto the pillow. Her sandy-brown locks bounced. He lifted her skirt, placed his large hands on her thighs, and spread her legs wide. He placed his tongue on her. She quivered. He moved slowly. She felt each tastebud on his tongue striking her. Her toes curled. He slid his tongue down, inside her. Her leg began to shake.

"Oh, damn. Oh, shit. Joshua."

He started to move his tongue faster. Her leg began to shake faster. She grabbed the back of his head. She squeezed his ears.

He began to roll his head in a circular motion. She moaned loudly.

"Okay. Okay, wait," she said, breathing hard. "Wait."

Joshua lifted his head. His mouth glistened.

"What's wrong?" He was out of breath, too.

"Nothing." Kathryn was glowing. "Nothing's wrong. I just want to return the favor."

They exchanged positions. He laid his head back on the pillow. She rubbed his stomach.

"Wow. You really have a nice body. You should show it off."

"I do? Thanks. That's not really my thing, though."

"Well, I guess you'll be my best-kept secret." She giggled.

She pulled his jeans down, then his underwear. Joshua felt her hot mouth on him. He took a deep breath. He looked down at her, amazed. She moistened him. He clenched his jaw. She looked up at him, and smiled.

XXX

The next day was homecoming and Diego was up bright and early, waiting for the festivities to begin. His white T-shirt was freshly pressed and crisp. His ponytail was slicked back.

"Josh. Joshua. Wake the fuck up, dude. Let's go to the caf'. Get some breakfast. It's a fucking beautiful day."

Joshua tossed in his bed.

"Dude, get the fuck up! What happened to you last night? Thought we were hitting the Black Hole? It was off the chain."

Joshua stirred again, then slowly opened his eyes.

"Man, why are you busting my balls? I hung out with Kathryn last night."

"Again? Damn. That's like, what, a month? And you still haven't fucked."

Joshua gave Diego a sly look. He reached over to his desk and grabbed his glasses.

"Shut the hell up. No, you didn't."

"Man. Wow. It was crazy."

"Shut up. Whatever."

Joshua smiled. He confidently rubbed his chin and gazed off into the distance.

Diego became intrigued.

"Damn. Are you serious? You hit that?"

Joshua smiled as wide as his face would allow.

"Damn! So you're not a virgin anymore."

"Dude, shut up. I wasn't a virgin."

Diego smirked.

"Uh, yeah, you are. Or were. Don't fake."

"Whatever. Anyway, man. It was crazy."

"So you fucked?"

"Well, not exactly."

"She gave you a dome shot?"

Joshua smiled.

"Wow! Nice. Look at my boy, growing up and shit."

"Dude, it was tight. And she didn't stop when I…you know."

"Damn! She drank the babies?"

"Like Jungle Juice."

"Wow! She's a keeper. You have a keeper right there. You need to go ahead and wife her."

Joshua smiled. Diego shook his head in amazement, then he paused.

"So it was good, huh? Man, you know, not to bust your bubble, but that probably means that wasn't her first time doing it. You do realize that, right?"

Joshua sat there for a moment. He pondered. He shifted his weight. He scratched his neck.

"I mean, you know. Whatever. Who cares, right? I'm with her now."

Diego leaned over and checked his goatee in the mirror on Joshua's closet.

"Yeah. Yeah, you right. Who cares? I'm happy for you, home boy." Diego stopped for a minute. "So what did you do? Did you eat it?"

Joshua was tying his shoelace when he suddenly stopped.

"Huh?"

"I said, did you eat it? You know, bite. You did, didn't you?"

Joshua smiled broadly.

"Oh! You're a beast, man! A true savage."

"I mean, I had to. I had to eat it. You know? It was just one of those things."

Diego laughingly pushed Joshua.

"I ain't mad at you. You did what you had to do. You're a hog!" He laughed again. "Man, that's wild. You ready to get something to eat, or what?"

XXX

After breakfast, Joshua and Diego walked out onto the yard. It was already filling up with students, parents, alumni, and people from the local towns. A kinetic energy overtook the small Southern campus.

"Man. Look at this," Diego said, using a toothpick to pick out a salty chunk of bacon. "It's a beautiful day. Not a cloud in the sky. Look at all these honies walking around. Man! I love being in college."

"Yeah, this is crazy. Looks like more people than last year." Joshua adjusted his glasses. "I think it's hotter this year, too. Looks like the girls are wearing less."

As he said that, a group of girls with tiny shorts strolled past. Catcalls and whistles and pick-up lines flew. They didn't stop walking.

"Man, did you see them? This is going to be a good day," Diego said, stroking his goatee. "Yo, I'm going back to the room to change my shorts, throw on my Jordans. You gonna be here or are you coming back to the room?"

Joshua was about to answer when he saw Kathryn and her roommate, Roxanne, walking toward the cafeteria.

"Uh, you go ahead. I'll be up here."

Diego noticed Kathryn walking up and he chuckled.

"Okay. Man, you sprung already? Whatever. I'll be back."

Joshua nodded to Diego. He couldn't control his smile when Kathryn spoke.

"Hey, handsome. What's going on?"

"Not too much. Just ate. What are you doing here?"

Kathryn and Roxanne laughed.

"Um, we're hungry, too," Kathryn said with a smile. "We came to eat, too."

"Duh," Roxanne added with a laugh. Her hair was dyed a vibrant red and cut low in the back. She was similar in size to Kathryn, though an inch or two taller.

"This is my roommate, Roxanne. We grew up together. This is Josh. Joshua."

"Hey."

"Hey to you. Look, ya'll can stand out here and talk but I'm finna eat 'fore the caf' closes. Excuse me."

Roxanne brushed past Joshua and sashayed into the cafeteria. Joshua frowned at her.

"It's crazy out here, right?" Joshua asked.

"It is. Look at all these people." Kathryn glanced out over the campus. The cafeteria was located directly in the middle of the yard, so they could see lines of cars coming in from all directions, flying State flags and playing loud hip-hop music. The sidewalks were jammed with pedestrians, young and old. Two guys walking past said hi to Kathryn. She didn't speak.

"And it's still early. Tonight is going to be really crazy," Kathryn said, shaking her head. "You want to come in the caf' with me?"

Joshua nodded and they walked inside. While heading to his dorm on the other side of campus, Diego ran into an old crush, one he never felt the fire of, but always wanted to. He said a few sweet things. She smiled. Feeling the joy of the day, she entertained him.

"Why don't you come up to the room for a second? My roommate is gone."

"You want me to sneak in?" she asked with a sugary, mousy voice. Her skin was light brown and extremely smooth. She was petite, too, just how Diego liked them.

"Yeah. It's nothing. See that door? Just post right there. I'm going in by the main door and I'll come around and open it. We can take the stairs up."

She seemed unsure.

"Hey. It's homecoming! Live a little."

She smiled.

"Okay."

XXX

"You had a good time last night?" Joshua asked while Kathryn dug into a plate of eggs. They were runny so she dashed on a heap of salt and pepper.

"I did." She chuckled. "Did you?"

"You know I did," Joshua said with a grin.

"What the hell are ya'll talkin' about? I seen *Friday*, too. It ain't that damn funny." Roxanne squirted ketchup on her eggs and fried potatoes.

Kathryn and Joshua smiled.

Out the corner of his eye, Joshua could see a guy walking up behind Kathryn. He'd seen him before. A buff guy who always wore tank tops. He had on a red one today. He tapped Kathryn on the shoulder.

"What's up, homie? Where you been at?"

Kathryn jumped. She looked up at him.

"Oh, hey." The fork in her hand gently shook. She looked uneasy.

"I've been around."

"Fasho. I'm saying, though. Missed you at the party last weekend. What you got up for later?"

"Probably hanging out with my boy, Joshua." She pointed across the table to Joshua. Roxanne ate her food with an amused smirk on her face.

"Oh, yeah?" The guy eyeballed Joshua.

"Yep," Joshua said. "And honestly, you kind of interrupted our conversation."

The guy was taken aback.

"Oh, it's like that?" He looked at Kathryn.

She nodded.

"Yeah, it is."

"Wow. Okay. Cool. Holla at ya boy," he said before stomping off.

"Thank you," Kathryn said. "He's a jerk."

"No problem," Joshua said. "He saw us talking. That was rude and disrespectful. For real."

"I know. Thank you."

XXX

The girls finished their breakfast and they walked outside with Joshua to bask in the festive heat of the mid-morning.

"Dude! I've been waiting for you to get out of there." Diego was cheesing. He had two plastic cups in his hands. "They wouldn't let me in without my ID card. It just went down in the room. Take this."

"What happened?" Joshua was curious. He took the cup and smelled the contents. Kathryn and Roxanne stood a few feet away talking.

"Don't smell it, buster. Just drink it. Anyway, snuck a little shorty up there. It popped off. Sorry, but I used your bed."

"What?" Joshua took a sip of the drink. It tasted like strawberries.

"Mine was all made up. I'll wash your comforter." Diego looked over at Kathryn. "Man, let's take a little stroll around the yard. Tell your girl we'll get with them in a few minutes."

Joshua chatted with Kathryn and she and Roxanne walked off. The fraternities and sororities were in full force all over campus. Several of the Greek organizations held coming-out ceremonies for their newest members. Others had events and parties planned for later that night. Joshua and Diego started a casual stroll through the crowd of people gathered in the streets and on the sidewalks. They sipped their beverages.

"I just wished I would have done more things, like pledge a fraternity, or join some clubs or something," Joshua said, eyeing a group of guys in red-and-white fraternity jackets.

"Man, fuck that shit. Who needs a fraternity? We fuck the same bitches, right?"

Joshua laughed. His glasses slid so he pushed them back up.

"Look," Diego said, while carefully scoping the yard. "Pretty soon you'll be an architect or some shit and I'll still be bangin' hot chicks. So it's all good."

Joshua laughed.

"This is true. Man, what is in this cup?"

Diego smiled.

"Oh, you like that? It's cisco. Liquid crack, baby. Enjoy."

"Dang," Joshua said, staring at his cup. He took another drink. "Oh well. It's homecoming!"

"Now that's how you do it!" Diego said.

They continued to walk through the crowd. Diego spoke to a few guys and girls he knew. Joshua secretly hoped he'd bump into Kathryn. Diego could sense something was on his mind.

"Man, what's up? What you thinking about?"

"Huh? Nothing."

"Nothing? Yeah, right. I've known you too long. You thinkin' about that broad."

"Huh? Whatever," Joshua said, about to scratch his neck.

"See! I knew it. The neck scratch. It's cool, dog. It's cool. Do ya thang."

Joshua grinned. He adjusted his glasses.

"Man, Diego. I do like her. Like, for real. What should I do?"

Diego took another swig.

"Shit. Just keep fucking her. What else is there to do?"

Joshua shrugged.

"I mean, I like her more than that. It's deeper than that. She's real cool, you know? Easy to talk to. Plus, she fun to hang out with."

Diego stopped to tie his shoe.

"Look, do ya thing. If you like her, make it happen. Don't trip on what anybody has to say. You feel me? Just go with it."

While Diego was kneeling on the congested sidewalk, one of the frat boys bumped into him, almost knocking him over.

"What the fuck?" Diego jumped up.

"Watch what the hell you're doing, G.D.I.!"

Diego was caught off guard.

"What? What did you call me?"

All the eyes on the sidewalk and street were suddenly on Diego, Joshua, and now about six or seven Betas who had gathered around.

"I called you a G.D.I. A Goddamn Individual. Watch who you're bumping into, chump."

Diego exhaled a calm breath. He looked over at Joshua. He looked timid. Diego didn't care. He turned back toward the Beta and sized him up. About the same size. Diego had more of a muscular build. *Fuck it*, he thought.

"Man, fuck you and the whole Beta organization." The crowd let out a collective groan.

"Come on, Diego!"

"Hell naw, cuz! These Betas want war? I'll take 'em to war! I ain't some punk-ass college kid!"

"What the fuck did you say?" the Beta asked. They all wore black-and-gold jackets.

"You heard me!"

"Yeah, you G.D.I.s just need to watch your mouths. You suckers wish you were Betas." The guy looked back at his fraternity brothers. "Let's go, fellas."

They all slowly walked off, ogling Joshua and Diego.

"Man, are you trying to get us jumped?" Joshua's heart was pumping fast. He could feel the effect of the liquor. "It was like ten of them."

"Whatever. I ain't no punk," Diego said, checking on his Jordans to make sure they were still white and clean. "Those cats know they haven't seen no parts of the streets. I'm from the 'hood. My people didn't go to college. I'm not the one to fuck with, for real. Don't let me call my boys about this. It'll really be on. Somebody won't be graduating, I'll tell you that. Do they really think I look like a sucka or something?"

"Man, that was crazy," Joshua said, looking through the crowd to see if they were coming back.

Diego laughed.

"Man, that was nothing. I can show those busters crazy."

Joshua laughed. Adrenaline was still flowing through his veins.

Suddenly Diego was bumped again, this time harder and more deliberately. The guy kept walking without looking back.

"Man, what the fuck? Is this Bump Fly-ass Diego Day?"

"Diego, man. Let it go." Joshua tried to calm him.

"'Let it go'? Fuck that. I'm from the block! Twice in a row? We don't let shit ride. I'm not letting this one go."

Diego stepped quickly toward the guy who had bumped him, weaving through the throng of people on the sidewalk and in the street.

"Diego, come on, man. Remember the Million Man March. Brothas got to stick together," Joshua said, fully meaning it.

Diego slowed his pace and turned to face Joshua.

"What? The Million Man March? Man, fuck that! Ya boy is about to get a million-block stomp-down. And that's on my momma."

Then Diego spotted him, talking to a group of guys. That didn't deter him.

"A, homeboy, you just bumped all into me and didn't say excuse me. I think an apology is in order."

"What you say, bruh?"

A small crowd started to gather around them. The other guy was taller and heavier than Diego, but he didn't care.

"I said, you bumped me. Least you could say is 'excuse me.'"

The guy smiled widely, exposing two rows of gold teeth.

"Look, bruh, you really need to keep it movin' with all that nonsense, bruh. Ya dig?"

Diego looked back at Joshua, who was feverishly scratching his neck. The brilliant midday sun was shining brightly. The crowd around them had ballooned. Girls and guys and even some parents stood by watching. Cars in the street slowed to a crawl when they noticed the crowd gathering.

"Keep it movin'? Okay, cuz." Diego slowly turned to walk away but quickly swung around and caught the guy with a punch to his chin, dropping his large body to the pavement.

In unison, the crowd let out an "ohhh!" Diego was pumped.

"Yeah! That's how Diego do it! Blaxican! Midwest! Take yo punk ass back to New Orleans, homeboy."

The guy lay on the ground, holding his face. Diego gave one more gesture of superiority, then turned to walk away.

"Diego!" Joshua yelled out.

But it was too late. Diego suddenly felt a piercing pain in his side, a deep, wrenching pain he had never felt before. He fell to his knees.

Joshua ran toward his friend. The guy Diego punched fled through the crowd, the knife still in his hand.

"Oh, fuck, cuz. Damn." Diego was feeling woozy. Blood poured from his body. He collapsed.

"Somebody, get an ambulance!" Joshua was frantic. He lifted Diego's head. "You're cool, man. You're good. Somebody, call 9-1-1!"

"Damn, dude. He fucking stabbed me. Shit, cuz. Is it bad? Am I bad?"

Joshua looked down. Diego's white T-shirt was now blood-red. A puddle was slowly forming under him.

"It's not bad, man. You're good. Somebody, get help!" Joshua tried to apply pressure to the wound but Diego yelled out in pain.

"Damn, cuz. It burns. But I'm cold, man. Fuck. I'm getting cold, Josh." Diego started to cry. "I'm dying, cuz. I'm dying. Oh shit. It's cold, man. Damn, Josh. He stabbed me. I'm getting cold. Why did he stab me?"

Two blocks away, an ambulance struggled to get through, sirens blazing. The congestion on the street and sidewalks made it nearly impossible. They blew the horn, but cars had nowhere to go. The campus was jam-packed for the weekend's events. The paramedics parked the ambulance and hopped out.

"Hold on, Diego. They're coming." Joshua was crying.

"Okay, man. Okay. I'm trying." Diego closed his eyes. "I'm trying. Told you it was a pretty day, man. But I'm tryin'. I'm tryin'."

Diego's body went still. The puddle of blood beneath him ran the length of his body.

"Diego? Diego!" Joshua squeezed him. "No. No, man. No."

xxx

A week later, Diego was laid to rest in his hometown. Joshua couldn't afford the trip home. So instead he spent the week in Kathryn's room. Unable to eat, unable to concentrate. Every night he had to duck the dorm mother, but it was worth that small hassle to feel the warmth of somebody who cared about him. She borrowed his car to drive into town and run errands with Roxanne. She and Roxanne got tattoos. She got snacks and movies for them to watch. He lay in the bed, missing classes. He got up the strength once to meet with his counselor. His instructors would freeze his grades where they were; the missed days would not be counted against him. The whole time he thought about the rest of his time at State. How could he do it? How could he go there without Diego, his friend since high school? He decided he couldn't.

The winter nights turned cold. He and Kathryn made love often. When she began talking about moving to D.C., to be closer to her father, Joshua was more than happy to entertain the notion. There was nothing keeping him at State. There was nothing tethering him to Aunt Trell. He decided to go with her at the end of the semester. They would load up his Toyota and make the drive. There was nothing keeping him there. He looked forward to starting a new life with his girlfriend, Kathryn.

CHAPTER 15

AUGUST 15, 2008
1:01 A.M.

Joshua swiftly lunged for her, but she, equally as fast, kicked him to keep him at bay. Kathryn swung wildly at Joshua. Shower curtain rings popped off as the two became entangled in rage and hate.

"All the years I've given you? All these years! You haven't worked! You just *are*!" Joshua screamed while tears welled up in his eyes and ran down his face.

"You cheated on me! I fucking hate you!"

Joshua snatched Kathryn's leg and pulled her as she continued to fight him, grazing his face with gnarled hands. She then stretched her fingers and began to dig her nails into his face.

Joshua yelled out from the stabbing pain and released her leg, searching for a towel to slow the bleeding while embracing his gashed face. Kathryn showed an expression of relief, as if she had just taken a long piss after hours of holding it. Joshua quickly found a towel and applied pressure to his bleeding face, and as he did so, he was surprised by the look of pleasant satisfaction on his wife's soaked face. *Such a sinister grin*, he thought, *flaunting a smile like that*. Even under the circumstances, the look was heartwrenching. He paused. Outside the window, he could see into the smiling night. Joshua once had a dream where he died. There was nothing. No heaven. No hell. No gates, pearly or otherwise. Just nothing. Tonight, he again felt that dead nothing.

"Darling. My darling Joshua. I used to love you, too," Kathryn whispered in sluggish speech. She again wiped the water from the left side of her face, the black swirl now a plunging streak defiling her pretty features. Her fingernails harbored chunks of skin like a butcher's cleaver.

"Why did you do these things to me, Kathryn? Why did you hurt me like this?"

Kathryn looked at him with hatred on her face.

"You don't think I hurt? You don't think I'm in pain?" Kathryn began to sob. "I'm in pain, Joshua. I'm in pain! So much pain. I wish I could curl up and die. Just close my eyes and disappear, Joshua. I didn't ask for this. It hurts so much. Don't you know that? My soul aches."

Joshua wiped his face.

"You killed our son, Kathryn! My beautiful baby boy!"

Kathryn scowled at him.

"You killed one, too. Remember that? Do you remember that, Joshua? Before we left State. I remember the day. You made me get a fucking abortion! You remember that?"

Joshua turned his head.

"We weren't ready for a kid," he said.

"Weren't ready? Weren't ready? I was ready! I was ready to have someone to hold and to have someone to talk to. I was ready!"

"And with Junior? Didn't you have him?"

Kathryn began to weep again, a small, child-like whimper.

"I don't know. I couldn't focus. I wasn't the same. After…after that day, I just couldn't focus. Couldn't think straight." She wiped her tears. "But what does it matter?"

She closed her eyes.

"You killed one. Now I've killed one. Guess we're even, now."

Threads of blood trickled beyond the towel through Joshua's index finger and thumb on the left, ring finger and pinkie on the right. A speck of the fluid neared the corner of his mouth. He tasted it with the tip of his tongue. It was salty. Suddenly, a new thought hit him like a crackle of mid-summer thunder: "How the fuck did we get here?"

Kathryn wouldn't let up.

"Yeah, I've done a few things that I'm not proud of, but are you perfect? You want to judge me? Go to hell, Joshua! Go to hell!"

Joshua felt his heart softening.

"Look at us, Kathryn. We're not the same. We were friends. What happened?"

"I don't know, Joshua. You cheated on me, remember?"

Joshua tilted his neck and heard a relieving popping sound.

"Yeah, I cheated on you. But you know what? You cheated on me first."

Kathryn looked confused.

"I've never cheated on you. You know, Roxanne thought I was stupid for dating you. The girls in my dorm said you were a geek, and goofy. Those weeks you stayed with me; I heard it all. But me, I thought you were a sweet, handsome guy. How can you say I cheated on you? I could have. I probably should have, just to test the waters. See what else was out there."

She leaned forward to try to get out of the bathtub, but her drunkenness and the weight of the water prevented it. She slouched back into the tub.

"You know, Kathryn, you know why I cheated on you? Because you fucking *did* cheat on me. Remember your little friend Blaine and 'Brooklyn'? You remember that fucking great time you had?"

Kathryn wiped the water from her face.

"I don't know what the fuck you're talking about." She looked around. "I'm getting out of this fucking bathtub, I do know that."

Joshua became angry and pushed her back down. Her limp body put up no resistance and slid back into the water.

"Goddamn it, Joshua! Let me out! I don't know what the hell you're talking about!"

"That tattoo, Kathryn. You didn't get that angel on your shoulder until after we started dating. After. Blaine said he had his hand all in it." Joshua lowered his head. "How could you do that? How could you do that to me?"

Kathryn let out a long exhale.

"Joshua, yes, you were there for me. And I was there for you. But...please, let me get out of this tub. I can't talk like this."

She stuck her legs out and sat on the side of the bathtub. Her soaked gown rained down on the floor.

"Why, Kathryn? Why?"

She took another deep breath.

"It was after Diego died. You...you were really down. You remember? I was there for you, too, right? I know I was. But I had needs. I had needs, too. Damn, Joshua. This might be the wine talking, but I was young. I wanted to live, to have fun. I guess I got drunk one night and things went too far. I don't know what else to say. I'm sorry. I didn't mean to hurt you. I still loved you. I still do."

She wiped her face again.

"I forgave you for what you did; that hotel thing. You should be able to forgive me, Josh. We can start over. Can you forgive me?"

Joshua looked up. Tears ran down his face.

"Joshua, can't you forgive me? That was a long time ago. We were young. We have a life together, now. A precious life. So I'm asking, can't you forgive me?"

Joshua wiped the tears from his face.

"No." He leaned closer to her. "I can't."

XXX

The weather the next evening was steamy and uncomfortable. Lightning bugs struck their bright chords and illuminated the small spaces they occupied. Runners jogged on the sidewalks and sweat poured from their foreheads. Families went for ice cream, and dogs frolicked off their leashes.

At the gym, the mood was solemn. By now most of the trainers had heard the news, some of the clients, too. The neighbors from Arkansas had heard the commotion last night and called the police. Many of the people at the gym toiled on, though, oblivious to the event. They dropped sweat on the machines. Performed exercises incorrectly, negating any positive effect their exertion might have had, wasting time under the guise of wellness. Their greed and abundance smothering them. Chidu quietly sat in Josh's old office, wiping away tears. Susan stumbled upon him.

"Hey, kiddo. I heard what happened. How you holding up?"

Chidu silently shook his head.

"I know. This is so sad. I know he was your friend," she said, gently rubbing Chidu's shoulder. "Who knew he was that angry at the world? It's a shame, truly. A sad shame."

Chidu nodded in agreement.

"So it looks like I'm in need of a trainer now. What do you think?"

Chidu gave her a puzzled look. He wiped his eyes.

"Well, think about it. I could use the help, kiddo. See you around. Hang in there."

Susan slowly walked away. Chidu looked at a photograph on Joshua's desk. He thought about their nights out drinking cold beer and flirting with pretty women. The office was quiet. He couldn't hear the whir of the stationary bicycles or the clatter of metal on metal. The silence encapsulated him. It became uncomfortable. He turned the television on.

"Well, Leon, pre-season sales of Redskins tickets are doing well, so well in fact, that tickets are already appearing on eBay and other auction sites. One fan who missed the opening-day sales while on vacation in Europe said no price is too much to pay, to see his beloved Redskins.

"'I've been to every opening home game since I was a little boy. No amount of money would keep me from holding true to my family's tradition that's continued with me and my two boys. Go Redskins!'

"There's no word from that fan yet whether or not he's been able to score tickets, Leon, but by the sounds of things, he seems pretty determined."

"Okay, thanks, Frank. An Alexandria couple and their niece were found dead last night after an apparent murder-suicide. Police have not released the identity of the slain, and they have yet to identify a motive. More news from Iraq. As the death toll continues to rise, what's being done to treat the mental conditions of survivors here in the States? More on that in a moment. Is it getting hotter out there? Bill Bellows is up next with the weather."

"That's right, Leon, it's getting hotter and more humid. Keep your water bottles and sunscreen handy. You'll want to hear how to keep safe under these stifling conditions. Stay tuned."

About the Author

Che Parker is the author of *The Tragic Flaw*. He has worked as a crime and politics reporter and staff writer covering national health care and Capitol Hill hearings. Currently a graduate student at Johns Hopkins University, he works in public relations and lives in Alexandria, Virginia. You may email the author at cheparker@hotmail.com

EXCERPT FROM

The Tragic *Flaw*

BY CHE PARKER
AVAILABLE FROM STREBOR BOOKS

Chapter 1

Youthful laughter permeates the old neighborhood on an unseasonably sultry winter day. Three-story homes and greening arbors line the streets on either side. The homes' aged and stately appearances clash with the sounds of adolescence. Older model cars dot College Avenue here and there. Most are well kept, washed and waxed, and parked close enough to the curb as to avoid the all too infamous sideswipe. Others lack hubcaps, or sport more than one tone—black and taupe, for instance—certainly not what the manufacturer intended.

Still others lack tires, or have been clasped with city-owned clamps that prevent them from doing what they're meant to do. Of course they're American made. Names like Buick, Ford, and Oldsmobile are commonplace. More than one flatbed truck lives here, and is used here, often to haul in bicycles that require assembly, or to haul out sofas when excuses no longer dissuade eager landlords.

The gold and red masonry of the homes stands strong in the face of frail innocence. The dwellings are seemingly paternal in essence, standing watch over tomorrow's dearest. Visible black bars of iron cover nearly every window on the ground level, hinting at unforeseen perils and dangers that might thrive in this community.

Most sidewalks are well swept, but a few could use sprucing up. They very often resemble the tidiness of the vehicles parked just in front of them. Wrappers with words like Coca-Cola, Jolly Ranchers, and Coors, and other colorful plastics with various titles are seen in gutters, not everywhere, but more than enough.

A single ringing gunshot is heard while children are at play. Nothing uncommon for this neighborhood, so the youth continue their games in the thick humid air. Some, mostly girls, are tossing rocks on quadrangles and hopping on unsteady feet. Others, sweaty boys in T-shirts and dirty blue jeans, thrust outstretched hands toward still others, boys and girls who flee as if their pursuers wished to transmit smallpox or leprosy. Several girls, not quite nubile, twirl opposing ropes as a single entrenched participant leaps in a battle against the encircling cords. Her laughter is infectious, as her beaded locks frolic about and sweat drips from her brow. They're clad in cut-rate shorts and tank tops with waning hues of pink and lavender, and off-white sandals that have had their fair share of rope jumping and inner-city jaunts. The other two partakers giggle with her and against her. They're not new to this game; they have played it many times. Each time it is pleasurable. The summertime weather beckons, even though it is only February. Another gunshot rings out, echoing against the urban edifices. There's still no reaction from the playing preteens as they chuckle and skip.

They have songs and chants and rhymes that usually accompany their rope exercise, but not this time. This time it's more serious. The middle combatant is a champion, and her compatriots wish to dethrone her. Even still, her feet seem to be magnetically repelled by the ground and the ropes. They smack the hot turf methodically while avoiding the merest brush with the composite twine.

A graying grandmother exits her front door and comes to sit idle on her stoop, observing the ever-changing world through wise, time-tested eyes. She has been a witness to Jackie Robinson's first base hit, lynchings, riots, and space travel. She's seen the persecution of quadroons and conversely, the invalidation of age-old taboos. She, perhaps unlike others her age, has no fear of dying.

Her faded floral housecoat and matching slippers appear as aged as she, and her brown, wrinkled, and calloused hands offer a glimpse into the difficult life she has led. Lovely roses of all colors begin to bloom in her yard, fooled by the early ninety-degree day. She has diligently tended to these flowers for years.

The glowing sun fights through the scattered clouds. Baby blue occupies the sky. Undeterred yellow beams of light strike the pavement. It is un-doubtedly a beautiful day.

A beam catches one young lass's light-brown eyes and long lashes, enhancing both, as she twirls her end of the two ropes with coffee-colored hands. Sweaty palms grasp the cordage as she fights to hold on.

Family gatherings bring the aroma of mesquite and charred beef and pork. Third generations are ordered to perform songs and dances for first generations. It's tradition on days like this. And with weather so lovely in the dead of winter, all wish to take advantage of it.

A badly lit mom-and-pop corner store sees a steady stream of at least three generations during the day and well into the night. The neighborhood's rambunctious kids are sustained with consistently stocked shelves of licorice and hot pickles.

Middle-aged and sturdy fix-it men in tattered coveralls stop by for D batteries, seventy five-watt light bulbs, nails, and flat-head compatible screws kept on dusty wooden racks. They chat briefly with the owner about how their home team could go all the way if they just had a decent secondary and some semblance of a pass rush. Well-known rummies fall in for the inexpensive lagers and two-dollar bottles of *vino* stored in lukewarm refrigerator units.

A cool breeze blows. A crackle of thunder interrupts the melodic chuckles, yet the play goes on. The flow of business at the bazaar is uninterrupted. A burnt-out drunk with a hardened face pours worthless suds from this empty beer bottle onto the sidewalk. He then asks the neighborhood's young hustlers for spare change, and they in turn laugh at him, as always. The abodes, while casting a regal shadow of protection on the area's most precious resource, hide a secret.

For just a few feet away, one turn to the left, a few paces down, and yet another swivel the opposite way, then down an alley where vermin reside and slime and sludge congregate, lies a dying shell. It is the shell of a man. The dying, bleeding shell of a man. That ringing shot was no accident. It has hit its mark.

Key aspects of his chest are absent. Maroon solution cascades down the side of his torso in a slow waterfall of despair and anguish.

Yet the children's laughter is still heard, ignorant that it fills the ears of the perishing, who is in no need of its sardonic prodding. The burgundy life force pools just beneath its reluctant spring. The giggling intensifies and is ubiquitous as the clouds open and it begins to rain. A mad scramble is made to every step, stoop, doorway, door, foyer, and elsewhere.

The stray yellow beams of light have been overwhelmed by the dark gray coming of the rain.

The relentless drops splash in the unsuspecting red sauce, pounding the man's body, which at this point has no say in the matter. Yet, sirens can be heard in the background. There is hope for him, as the rain pours. The sudden precipitation makes an overwhelming *SSSHHHH* sound as it coats everything in what appears to be insurmountable moisture.

The man wears exquisite garb from the Old World. Fine lines, evenly stitched, and thread counts in the hundreds, position themselves along sinewy flesh. The stench of forthcoming death lingers as his eyelids flutter. His breathing is weak and faint.

The brilliant powder-blue mainstay of his soaked shirt contrasts sharply with poignant crimson lines that intersect throughout it. Midnight-colored trousers, also of the Italian peninsula, rest comfortably on the drenched and ever more dampening pavement. The man's slip-on onyx loafers lie fixed in a conflicting state, pointing directly at each other in a supple and unsightly way.

Zeus is restless. The rain pounds it all. The man's black blazer now functions as a colander for heaven's tears. His earth-tone hands and fingers, furrowed by the wetness, are bent in awkward positions. The fingers twitch as if communicating via sign language prior to what looks like an inevitable trip to the spirit world. His eyes become securely closed, looking as if he is simply napping as the sirens get louder and closer. The lines on his face display a few years, but not many.

He would look peaceful, if it weren't for his contorted posture and weather-beaten exterior. His frame becomes cold, losing any inkling of heat or energy. Rivers of waste and other remnants are washed to the man by the driving rain.

Rubbish, like shattered glass held together by sticky labels, begins to gather near his feet. Used condoms collect fittingly near his midsection; his body locked in a fetal position. All things urban are flushed toward this once proud man, who now finds himself a filter for a city's precipitation and refuse.

And still, the blood pours. It gathers, and then is dispersed by the rain into several streams that flow down the black glossy alleyway in an artistic display. It is fluid artwork that has decorated ghettos the world over. This medium, unlike colored pencils or pastel chalk, is the medium that keeps Hell engorged with uncaring youth and malevolent adults.

An expiring heart pumps faintly in a rain-soaked alley.

But blaring sirens near. All is not lost.

Chapter 2

Bullion barbs, approximately one hundred symmetrically aligned, millimeters in width, protrude from a focal point of gold. The entire mass rotates and reflects the radiant sunlight of the cloudless day.

The twenty-four-inch disk is accompanied by three clones in flanking positions, as they all support the weight of a large, pearl-white sport utility vehicle and its driver, currently en route.

The rotation of the SUV's Ohio-made rims is hypnotic. Nothing that big should be that gold. The oyster exterior is luminous. Not a speck nor smudge defiles its brilliance.

Its large black tires hug the Thirty-First Street concrete intimately, as if a love affair had been brewing since the new model left the showroom floor.

The driver is ever vigilant of potholes, swerving carefully to avoid them.

The scenery is bleak. Urban blight festers. Names crossed out in graffiti mark the deceased. On any given day, gunplay can make this place look like the Gaza Strip, or some Israeli settlement on the outskirts of the West Bank, except there's no "Breaking Coverage," no Wolf Blitzer, and no international outcry. Regardless, cashaholic militants carry out an assortment of transactions and will not hesitate to let Teflon-coated lead fly with the fervor of religious zealots. They'll die for this shit.

Corner after corner, someone's uncle chugs cheap wine and cheaper beer in an attempt to drown his sorrows, but in the ghetto they know how to tread water well. This while someone else's sister solicits every other blue-collar Joe and white-collar Jonathon.

"Hey! Hey, baby!" one clad in cherry hot pants screams to the SUV's driver, trying to flag him down. Her hazel eyes and delicate skin are appealing, but he's focused, and her call goes unnoticed.

The driver's path is fixed. Avenue after avenue, he continues without making a single turn, avoiding stray dogs and children fresh from summer school on this late June day. Empty brick buildings with broken windows abound.

There are signs of commerce, though. Aside from the open-air cash dealings for illegal narcotics, liquor stores, fast-food restaurants, pawnshops, pager shops, and check cashing businesses flourish here.

Residents of this once up-and-coming middle-class community poison their livers with fermented fruits and vegetables, then continue the self-imposed genocide by poisoning their bellies with high-fat, high-calorie fare. It's readily available and a little too convenient.

And yet the gold rims keep spinning.

The driver, clean-shaven and bald, sips expensive cognac from a red plastic cup. Bass lines from rap music send vibrations throughout the truck's peanut butter leather interior, causing the rear view mirror to shake and shimmy.

His tiny metallic digital phone rings. He grabs it from the center console, looks at the device's caller identification box, notices the number, and decides not to answer it, tossing it onto the passenger seat.

He takes another sip of his aged libation, hints of vanilla and oak escaping from the cup.

"Uuhh," he says, as his full lips curl. The drink is strong, but it's good.

Life in this neighborhood is enough to make anybody drink cordials during the middle of the day, the driver thinks to himself.

After making a right turn on Jackson Avenue and cruising several blocks, the driver pulls in front of a home and stops. He steps out of the truck. His light-blue alligator boots gently kiss the pavement. His blue, short-sleeved Australian-made sweater is intricately woven into eye-catching patterns. It matches his boots to a tee, as well as the picturesque sky above.

He crosses the street and comes before a white, one-story gated house watched by several surveillance cameras. It is extremely clean and well kempt, especially for this part of town.

He pushes a buzzer on an intercom. His diamond-encrusted, European-made watch glimmers in the sunshine. The princess cuts catch and display every color in the rainbow with their many facets. It seems to say, *bliiiing*. The time is 4:06 p.m.

A low male voice answers the driver's page, and asks professionally over the intercom, "Who is it?"

"Cicero," the driver answers, as he takes another sip from his plastic cup.

With a loud buzz, the gate, pulled by a rusty chain, begins to open, retracting to the left.

Cicero slowly walks in, and the gate begins closing behind him, making an obnoxious clanking noise. He takes one last swig of his auburn beverage and discards his red cup right in the front lawn. There's nothing else in the yard, and the cup stands out in the manicured emerald grass.

The electronic eyes follow his progress from the gate to the covered porch. Bars cover the windows.

Men's voices can be heard, muffled, emanating from within the house. The door is unlocked. Knowing this, Cicero turns the brass knob and walks in.

The place smells like a mixture of rancid marijuana smoke and fruity air fresheners plugged into the outlets, but it is immaculate.

White coats everything: white carpet, a white leather sofa and matching loveseat, white stereo equipment, a white marble-based coffee table with a glass top. Yet the stylish purity clashes subtly with the black African art that decorates the walls, not to mention the mannish and outlandish speech coming from a back room.

One rendering, framed in black wood, hangs above the sofa and features a black, bare-chested tribesman embracing his African queen, whose full breasts are exposed. It's huge, running the length of the long white sofa. In the background is the enchanting Serengeti. The chiseled sunburned peaks in the distance further emphasize the softness of the tribesman's bronze female.

Cicero eyes it, as he has many times, and just for a split second longs to be the man in the painting.

A sculpture of a woman stands nearly four feet and is situated to the left of the loveseat near a long hallway. The full figure and bouffant tresses give away the piece's ethnicity as its back arches and its hands are raised toward heaven as if giving praise to the Almighty.

A black-and-white still shot of Billie Holiday with her signature botanical adornment hangs over the love seat. The framed work beautifully depicts the elegant songstress' defined cheekbones, fine lips, and long flirtatious lashes. Her spread fingers, reacting to the heart-pounding offbeat jazz rhythms, make her hands appear to be in flight. Her lace-trimmed blouse is billowy. She is floating.

Mirrors, lined with white accents, are everywhere. The image of the large oil painting of the loving couple is bounced back and forth all over the wide living room, as is that of our elongated inanimate lady.

Cicero bends down and removes his boots, placing them right next to a pair of brand-new sneakers. This Japanese-based tradition of shoe removal, as requested by the homeowner, is a sign of respect. It is also what keeps the carpet the color of pure cocaine. Tan work boots and colorful tennis shoes line the wall to the left of the front door all the way to the towering white entertainment center that holds the state-of-the-art stereo system (also white) and the corresponding flat-screen plasma television.

"Shoot the fucking dice," one man says as Cicero walks down the hallway to the source of the hostility. His white socks blend perfectly into the plush Berber carpet, leaving size eleven footprints in his wake.

Cicero enters a back bedroom that has been converted into a recreation room of sorts. Five men occupy it. Four are kneeling. It's a crap game.

High stakes. Three thousand gets you a side bet. Four thousand gets you in the game.

"Man, will you stop shaking the fuckin' dice and just shoot," one heavily tattooed man says to another who also bears ink, in a frank and quite unfriendly tone. Twin jade serpents intertwine on his right forearm. His hair is tightly braided in straight parallel lanes.

"Chill out, mothafucka," the young dice holder says as he jostles the red die in his right hand. His left supports the weight of his kneeling body. "The sooner I shoot them the sooner you lose your money, asshole, so you better be happy I'm taking my fuckin' time," he says with a sinister smile on his face, exposing the gold and diamonds in his mouth. A Spanish inscription in Old English letters runs permanently down the back of his left arm: *El Hijo del Diablo*.

"Come on, mothafucka, I got shit to do," says another larger man in a black T-shirt, who has an intricate dragon with red eyes and green highlights spanning from his arm all the way up to the middle of his neck. He's extremely overweight.

One man is silently kneeling, looking on with intense eyes, hundred-dollar bills crumpled in his hand. An ink-inscribed name, "V-Dog," written in cursive letters, draws attention to the bulging bicep on his right arm. He has more than ten tattoos: names, abstract patterns, animals.

His dark-blue denim jeans and matching button-down shirt are heavily starched. His creases are rigid. He briefly glances up at Cicero with cold dark eyes, then looks back at the inactive dice holder.

Besides the men, the room is empty; half of it is uncarpeted, exposing hardwood parquet floors. It's perfect for tumbling dice. A very small stereo speaker pokes out of the wall near the door. The underground hip-hop music is tremendously clear, not too earsplitting.

The man with the rhombus crystals obscuring his teeth gives the dice one last good shake, then lets them fly out of his hand. They crash against the bottom of the wall, near the corner, and slide back toward the gambling quartet. One die stops before the other, showing three ecru circles. The second continues to roll, brushes one man's foot, then stops, displaying a total of…

"Seven," the shooter yells with excitement, quickly grabbing twelve thousand dollars and sweeping it behind him into an already large, mint-green pile becoming ever more virescent by the minute.

"Fuck," the large man says, as he reaches into his pocket for a fresh four thousand to get back into the game. The shooter is hot, and his three opponents are down a total of twenty-four thousand dollars.

"I'm out," says V-Dog. He's disgusted and feeling nauseous. He had planned on breaking everybody else and copping some soft. Now he's the broke one, and T.J., the lucky-ass dude with all his money, is talking shit.

"What's wrong, V-Dog?" the fresh-faced T.J. asks. "You all out of dough?" Everyone else in the room laughs.

V-Dog just looks at him, expressionless.

"Check it out, I'll front you four gees so you can stay in the game, V-Dog," a grinning T.J. says, and adds, "with one hundred fifty percent interest, mothafucka!" The room again erupts into laughter.

V-Dog looks unamused, and the other three men continue the game without him.

A fifth, dark-skinned man dressed in all black sits in a white, modern, art-deco half-moon chair. He's the homeowner. He looks up at Cicero and gives him a cool nod.

"Hey, what's up with you, Warren?" Cicero asks with his deep voice as he begins to count out three-thousand dollars so he can get some side bet action.

"Just chillin', man," Warren responds. "Tryin' to maintain."

"I heard that," Cicero replies.

He's feeling lucky, and T.J., his friend, is on fire. So why not bet on him, Cicero thinks.

T.J. rolls the dice again. No seven, but it's still a good roll.

"What's your point ,T.J.?" Cicero asks.

"What's crackin', C? My point eight, and I'm straight," he answers with a smile. His mouth brightens the room in a burst of light and sparkles.

"I bet he hits that eight," Cicero says to Warren, and as he does, he hears a dog barking loudly from outside.

Cicero, looking puzzled, says to the homeowner, "I didn't know you had a pit."

Warren, who isn't shooting dice, just observing, laughs. It's low and brief. He takes a puff from his freshly rolled joint.

"I don't," he says, exhaling a plume of thick cannabis smoke.

Cicero looks even more confused. Surely he has a pit bull, he ponders.

Warren then slowly rises out of his chair with a slight grunt. His potbelly weighs him down, but his jewel-encrusted timepiece makes him look like royalty. The chrome face, with its sweeping second hand, is flooded with yellow baguettes, and aquamarine sapphires surround the perimeter. He gets to his feet and walks out the room, motioning for Cicero to follow.

He does.

They walk through the bare kitchen to a back door. Warren slips on a pair of raggedy, navy-blue house shoes and opens the deadbolt lock with a key retrieved from deep within his jeans pocket.

The light-brown pine door opens and Cicero eyes the most massive canine he has ever seen.

"It's a Presa Canario," Warren declares, smiling proudly. "Fuck a pit bull."

The two step outside and proceed closer. Warren jokingly slaps the dog's huge head side-to-side while Cicero observes from a few feet away.

The animal resembles a prehistoric mammal that time forgot, a distant cousin of the saber-toothed tiger. Its muscular frame looks cartoonish, almost fake. But in its large square, fish-like mouth, reside very real teeth, and enough pressure per square inch to crush a lead pipe.

It snaps at the overly playful Warren, almost removing a finger.

The dog, panting heavily, is chained, but its jaw-dropping physique makes the steel chain seem like an inadequate restraint. Its chocolate coat glistens as white foamy drool flows past its thick black lips and down its chin. Its robust frame helps to conceal dark-red eyes. The ears, set high on its head, ironically resemble flower petals.

"Damn," Cicero mutters in a low voice.

"It's a boy, and I got his papers," comments Warren, who is now on one knee lovingly caressing the beast's head. "I'm looking for a female right now so I can breed 'em."

The dog looks Cicero directly in the eyes, causing him to take a small footstep back.

"Man, if you hear anything about a female for sale, let me know—" Warren says, finishing his sentence abruptly. He's cut off by arguing, and then a commotion, coming from inside his pristine home.

Cicero, hearing the ruckus, turns around to face the house as if expecting something strange or out of the ordinary to appear before him.

Bang! Bang! Bang! Bang! Bang! Five quick shots are heard, followed by the sounds of frantic scurrying. Cicero quickly pulls a nickel-plated revolver from his waistline and heads toward the back entryway. But before he can dart into the house, Warren yells to him, "Look out, C!"

With that, Warren releases the latch from his monster's collar. "Eat them mothafuckas up!" he yells to his instantly fanatical mongrel.

Warren's dazzling watch becomes shrouded in dirt and dust as the beast charges full speed toward the door. No longer barking, the only sounds heard from the creature are pants of rage and its huge paws pounding the earth.

Cicero leaps out of the way, as the beast would have certainly trampled him to reach his target. The front door slams and Warren's loyal animal begins barking loudly from inside the house.

Warren and Cicero cautiously enter. Cicero's weapon is cocked and ready to explode.

The two peer into the back room that several moments earlier was the venue for an urban sporting event. Now a dying body lay facedown on the hardwood floor, blood spewing from several new cavities. It's T.J.

Part of his head is missing. The once intact cranium has been splattered into bloody chunks all over the room, a grotesque ambiance. Active nerves in his body cause it to twitch. It is a disturbing sight.

Warren's loyal dog has his two front paws pressed against the front door, whining. His meal escaped.

"Damn, T.J.," Cicero says in a saddened tone. He looks over at the dice.

One is flat, clearly showing two small off-white circles. The other cube is diagonally propped up, wedged between the wood floor and the carpet, equally displaying five dots on one side, and one dot on the other. The fateful roll was obviously a bone of contention; one that ended young T.J.'s life. He was nineteen.

Blood squirts out of his carcass' various outlets. His white T-shirt now resembles a cape used in bullfighting. His ill-gotten winnings have vanished.

Warren is appalled at the sight before him.

"Look at my fucking carpet," he fumes. The blood has seeped into his flawless floor covering, leaving it a rosy pink. He stoops down over the body and gets a closer look, careful not to step into any of T.J.'s leaking juices.

"Man, why did he have to die like this?" Cicero asks out loud, but to no one in particular. He stands in the doorway.

Attila, Warren's furry companion, has made his way to the back room. The dog is more subdued now. It noses about the room, smelling the corpse and its bloodshed.

Cicero looks to Warren and asks, "You ever wonder how people end up in certain situations?"

Warren just glances up at him, disbelief written all over his fat bearded face. He offers no answer and his eyes return to the body and the blood.

Attila, who has begun to salivate, starts to lap at the blood. His thick tongue twists as it catches the liquid that is now beginning to coagulate on the oak wood floor as well as the white carpet. The beast savors the salty flavor.

"Stop! Stop, mothafucka!" Warren screams to his dog, forcefully yanking on its collar, barely budging the mammoth brute. "Stop! That's some nasty shit, Attila." He's finally successful in tearing his parched dog away from the solidifying pool of blood. Cicero just stares at the scene.

Warren massages the head of his Hershey-colored dog, staring in its eyes. "That mothafucka could have West Nile virus or some shit," he says in a concerned parental voice. "Now you got it, dummy."

Attila's head lowers as if he knows he has disappointed his master. Warren shakes his head, showing obvious displeasure in his canine's choice for a thirst quencher.

Countless thoughts run through Cicero's mind as he continues to gawk at T.J.'s bleeding body. But one sticks.

"You truly are the devil's son now," he says. "I guess."

The bearded Warren, now fully dismayed by the situation that has unfolded in his home, stands to his feet, strokes his face, and walks out of the room toward the front door. Attila trots out of the room and plops down on the fluffy white living room carpet and begins licking his balls.

"A, C, come here," Warren yells to his associate, who is still staring at T.J.'s corpse in the back of the house.

Cicero regains his composure and saunters out of the room. He's focused once again.

"One second," he says as he goes to the kitchen, opens the near-empty fridge, and grabs a cold imported beer with a German-sounding name. After quickly popping the top off the green bottle, he takes a much-needed swig then walks out of the kitchen toward Warren and asks, "What's up?"

"Check this out," Warren says, pointing to the dwindled row of footwear near the door.

Cicero notices just two pairs of shoes remain: his gators, and a brand-new pair of navy-blue sneakers. They would nicely complement a cobalt denim outfit. Apparently, their owner left with great haste.

Enunciating every letter, in a low menacing voice, Cicero confidently says the shooter's name: "V-Dog."

He ponders his next move for a moment, then remembers a booster is coming by his condo with some handmade Swiss timepieces she got with her five-finger discount.

"Yo, I got some business to attend to, Warren," Cicero says. "Be safe. And clean that shit up."

Warren shakes Cicero's hand as he leaves out, then cracks open the cell phone on his hip. He punches one number on speed dial. It is immediately answered.

"Hey, we have a plastic bag situation," he notes calmly.

"I'm on my way," the male voice on the phone says, just as relaxed, if not cooler. He hangs up, cutting off the blaring reggae music in the background.

In roughly fifteen minutes T.J.'s body will never be seen again. The process of dumping bodies is an American tradition, a ritual free of dishonest eulogies, all-black attire, and sobbing mothers. It is a Kansas City tradition.

A dirt hole in the outskirts of town now awaits young T.J.'s remains.